Thanks go to Rachel Levine and Joan Moran of Audace, Inc., for believing in me; to Jennifer, Dorothy, and the crew at Clarion for making it happen; to the friends who offered ideas and support, especially Nicole Bonilla, and to the Maya of yesterday and today. Most of all, thanks to Sharon and Edward Eboch, for parental support above and beyond the call of duty.

Clarion Books
a Houghton Mifflin Company imprint
215 Park Avenue South, New York, NY 10003
Text copyright © 1999 by Chris Eboch
Illustrations copyright © 1999 by Bryan Barnard

The text is 12/15-point Adobe Caslon.

Printed in the USA.

Library of Congress Cataloging-in-Publication Data
Eboch, Chris.
The well of sacrifice / by Chris Eboch.
p.   cm.
Summary: When a Mayan girl in ninth-century Guatemala suspects that the High Priest sacrifices anyone who stands in the way of his power, she proves herself a hero.
ISBN 0-395-90374-2
1. Mayas—Juvenile fiction. [1. Mayas—Fiction.
2. Indians of Central America—Fiction.
3. Human sacrifice—Fiction.] I. Title.
PZ7.E1945We 1999
[Fic]—dc21   97-31885
CIP
AC

MV   10   9   8   7   6   5   4   3

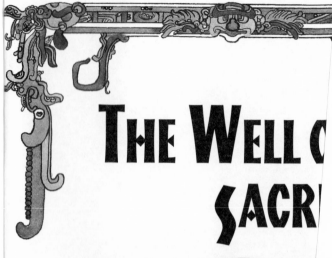

THE WELL OF SACRI

BY CHRIS EBOC

Illustrated by Bryn F

CLARION BOOKS · Ne

To Edward and Sharon Eboch
—C.E.

For my parents, who first showed me the land
of the Maya, *and for Sam,* whose generosity made the
illustrations in this book possible
—B.B.

ven in the middle of a clear day, much of the jungle is as dark as a room at dusk. Only a tiny amount of light filters through the layers of trees that rise to dizzying heights above the ground, higher than our tallest temples. The lack of light means little undergrowth can survive, so the walking is easy despite the enormous tree trunks and twisting vines. Ferns, mosses, herbs, and orchids grow on tree branches to be closer to the sunlight, and climbing vines twine around trunks and branches, forming knots and loops sometimes tight enough to strangle the tree.

In open areas where more sunlight reaches the ground, such as the edges of the jungle and near the river, bushes and herbs grow thick. The walking is harder, but I can gather more plants without a difficult climb to reach them.

Few girls go into the jungle, especially alone, as I have done so many times, but I know the jungle well, better than I know my own city. My mother and aunt, who were healers, often gathered medicinal herbs, roots, and seeds in the jungle, and my mother carried me with her when I was an infant. Later I worked at her side. I enjoyed those times, but I was forced to grow up quickly during the War with the Savages.

The Maya often fight with their neighbors and sometimes with foreigners, but this war was unlike any in the memories of the oldest men. The Savages came from the east and swept through the land, attacking small villages, burning crops, and sometimes even killing women and children. They moved quietly, in small bands, taking the villages by surprise, stealing what they could, and destroying the rest before vanishing into the jungle.

Our city prepared to battle with them many times, but when our warriors reached the village where the strangers had been, they found only smoking fields and villagers weeping over their dead families. For two years this continued, one village attacked, then quiet for a while, until people began to relax, and then another attack. The strangers had not yet dared come close to our city, which was too large and well guarded for their kind of fighting, but we suffered still.

Traders like my father, Eighteen Rabbit, suffered because the villagers could not afford their wares and traveling to other kingdoms was dangerous. Widows, orphans, and farmers who had lost their land poured into the city, needing food, clothing, and shelter. The storehouses, once overflowing with grain and goods collected through taxes for the use of the nobles and the needy, were almost empty. Since many villages could no longer pay their taxes, little food came in to replace what was used. The king asked for more from the farmers who had not been attacked, but it had been a dry year, and the ground will yield only so much grain.

Some of the villagers were sick when they came, and with so many people crowded close together and not enough healers, the illness spread. My mother, Blue Quetzal, and my aunt, Macaw Water, did all they could.

During the second year of the war, Macaw Water began treating a peasant family with bad coughs. One of the daughters, Moon Zero Bird, was about my age. I was supposed to keep out of Macaw Water's house, where evil spirits were at work in the sick people, but Moon would sit at the doorway and talk with me while I sorted and prepared medicinal herbs in the courtyard. She was excited about being in the city for the first time, and I promised to show her around as soon as she was better. She wanted to see everything, the temples, the market, the handsome young warriors and the beautiful noblewomen. She had never been away from her farming village before.

Macaw Water gave Moon and her family pudding pipe tree for the coughs and fever, mixing in a little cornmeal and vanilla for flavor. She also burned incense for healing; the sweet, spicy smell drifted into the courtyard while I worked. Nothing helped. Moon's family didn't seem terribly sick at first, but despite my aunt's efforts, they didn't get better. Moon's little brother was the first to die, then her two sisters. Moon was too sick to sit up anymore, but I talked to her from outside the doorway, reminding her of all the wonderful things we were going to do, if only she got better.

Moon died during the night. My mother told me in the morning, laying her arm gently across my shoulders, and then leaving me to cry in private. Moon had been one of my first real friends. Her father died next, and then her last brother. When they had all gone, her mother followed willingly.

Then Macaw Water got sick. She took to bed, tended by her eldest daughter. Soon the whole family was sick. Only a small courtyard separated our two houses, but my mother would not allow me to cross it to see my dying cousin, for fear of the evil spirits ravaging their house.

We buried my aunt and uncle with their four children under the stones of the courtyard. We all helped dig the graves, but Mother prepared the bodies by herself, placing cornmeal and a jade bead in each mouth so they would have food and money in the afterlife, then wrapping the bodies in cotton shrouds and sprinkling them with red cinnabar ore. We placed their tools and utensils, plus jewelry and offerings of food, around the bodies in the graves before covering them with stones.

After we sent her sister on to the otherworld, Mother confined herself to their empty house for a week, praying to the gods and conducting rituals to ward off the evil spirits. She made the rest of us stay away and out of danger. We joined her mournful wailing from across the courtyard.

Mother's spirit was strong. She didn't get sick and was soon busy again tending war victims. In the marketplace, prices rose, especially for food and medicine. Mother was too busy to gather medicinal herbs and plants, and neither she nor her patients could afford to buy enough, even when they were available. So the task fell to me.

My sister might have gone with me, as she was older, but she hated the jungle and refused. Feather Dawn insisted that her weaving, which was already very good, would bring in enough money to be a better help. Her fine clothes were popular with the nobles, but she would have made more money in times of peace, when cotton was not so scarce and people had more time and money to spend on clothes.

I was a child, ten years old, but I began to gather medicine on my own, following the methods I had learned from my mother and my aunt. I had to walk half the morning just to reach the jungle, passing through farmlands to the rough mountains that rose like a giant city from the plains. Even the lower foothills had been stripped of their trees by young men who came to gather firewood and carry it to the city on their backs. I scrambled over the dying stumps and small scattered plants before venturing just a little way into the edge of the jungle to look for palm nuts, pudding pipe tree, snakeroot, morning glory seeds, and pom resin from the copal tree.

One steamy, hot day in late spring, I wandered farther into the jungle than usual, trying to get away from the acrid, gritty smell of burning by the farmers clearing new land nearby. The smoke from the trees and plants filled my lungs with soot and seemed to dim the sun, but it released fresh cropland from the embrace of the jungle. They had begun farming on the lower slopes of the mountain itself, awkwardly cutting terraces into the uneven ground—they needed whatever land they could salvage. They could only grow crops in the same ground for three or four years before the soil turned bad.

I passed a rubber tapper at work. He began his rounds by dawn, before I reached the forest, cutting diagonal slashes into the trunks of wild rubber trees and fixing a little cup at the base of the cut to catch the milky sap as it drained. I saw him as he returned on his second round to pick up the sap, and we smiled and nodded briefly at each other. On my return to the city I might pass the thatched huts where the rubber tappers dripped the milky sap onto a stick held over a smoky fire, slowly building a great ball of rubber that they could sell in the market.

I continued deeper into the jungle. My mother was in desperate need of rabbit fern, which she used to cure poisonous animal bites. She thought it might help the infected cut on the arm of a pregnant farm woman. I finally found a patch of the ferns and was digging out the lumpy, reddish brown base of the third one when some sound above the distant screams of howler monkeys caught my attention. Then a bird shrieked a wild caw of alarm in the jungle canopy overhead.

I froze, crouched down amid the plants, scolding myself for carelessly forgetting the dangers of the jungle. Now I could only wait and hope that whatever beast made the sound would pass by without noticing me. A jaguar or puma would surely smell the sweat that dripped down my back, but perhaps this was only a fox or anteater.

Then I heard the sound of a man's voice. I released my breath. It was only one of the rubber tappers. I had frightened myself needlessly. I was about to rise, but I hesitated a moment more. What had the man said? His voice was strange somehow. I strained to hear a murmured answer, but the words made no sense to me. Puzzled, I waited, unsure what to do.

A man came into view through the brush around me, and then another. They were not Maya.

They were thinner then most Mayan men, with lighter, more yellowish skin. They had round, flat faces with short, straight foreheads. They didn't look very threatening, dressed only in breechcloths and sandals, with their hair cut short, but still the fear rose in my throat.

These were the Savages.

They paused nearby, a large group of them, chattering softly in a strange language. My calves began to burn from the awkward position I was in, but I dared not move. A few began to drink from gourds slung at their waists, and I saw one gourd painted with a design common to our people.

They seemed to reach a decision, and they all sat down. They took food out of the bags they carried: bananas, papaya, and nuts that they must have gathered as they walked. A small young man, who was seated closest to me, turned slightly away from the others. He slipped something out of his bag and ate it with his hand covering it so the others would not see. The man to his right noticed the strange actions and grabbed the small man's hand to see what he held. It was a strip of dried fish or meat, and the small man grinned and shrugged as the others began to yell at him.

A man with a fierce scowl and a necklace of copper

beads, probably stolen from some Mayan village headmaster, quieted the others. He made Small open his bag, but they found no more meat. Arguments broke out again, this time in low voices.

Sweat dripped from my forehead and slid alongside my nose, and mosquitoes landed on my skin, searching for the perfect place to bite. Tiny ants crawled over my feet. My nose began to tickle, and I carefully reached up to hold it, afraid I would sneeze. I worried that the men would stay there all day. But Necklace, who seemed to be the leader, reached a decision. They gathered up their belongings and started off toward the river. Small lingered, perhaps so the others wouldn't attack him from behind.

I began to relax. I tried to shift my weight, but I had lost all feeling in my legs. I tumbled over, sprawling onto my side in the ferns and letting out a gasp.

I waited in the silence that followed, my eyes shut tight. When I found the courage to open them, I saw Small staring down at me.

Our eyes locked.

I waited.

He said something I couldn't understand. When I didn't answer, he said it again.

"I don't understand," I told him.

He stared at me a moment, then nodded with a smile. He couldn't understand me either, but that in itself made my meaning clear.

Someone from the group ahead shouted. Small turned to answer. I tried to jump up and run, but my numb legs gave out and I collapsed in a heap.

Small turned back curiously. He saw the rabbit fern hearts I had unearthed. He pointed at them and seemed to ask a question. I handed one to him. He studied it, then bit into it. The tough root didn't appeal to him, so he handed it back with puzzlement. Then he smiled, turned, and walked away.

I watched his back disappear through the trees. When he was out of sight, my breathing slowed and I finally noticed the burning tingle that had overtaken my legs. It was so painful that tears poured from my eyes, and I could only lie there and wait until it passed.

Finally, I was able to stand. I tucked the three rabbit fern hearts into my bag and began to run for home, wobbly at first, then gaining speed. I didn't stop once, not even when I saw a poisonous coral snake in my path. I just leaped right over it.

When I finally broke out of the jungle, I didn't stop running. I sped on through the seemingly endless farms and peasant huts at the outskirts of the city. I stumbled, panting, past the larger houses of the merchants, until I reached the communal house where my brother lived. Girls were not allowed in such places, but I raced in anyway, yelling hoarsely for Smoke Shell.

Five young men looked up from the gambling game they were playing and stared at me. Smoke Shell had been about to throw the corn kernels painted with black marks, hoping to win the bet on how they would fall. He gently put them down, rose, and came to me. He took my arm and steered me solemnly out of the house.

"Eveningstar Macaw," he said, using my full name as he rarely did. "What has happened?"

I was panting for breath and so frantic to tell him that I could not speak. Sweat ran down my arms and legs.

"Is it Father?" he asked calmly, but with worry. I shook my head. "Mother is all right?" I nodded.

"Men. In jungle," I gasped.

"Stop. Take a few deep breaths."

I did as he said, and he waited patiently until I could talk sensibly.

"I was in the jungle gathering rabbit fern. I saw the Savages!"

"How many?"

I didn't know how to count. I thought wildly.

"As many as in your house and another."

"About twenty, then."

I nodded, though the number meant nothing to me. "One of them saw me, but he let me go. He didn't tell the others."

"Where was this?"

"They were heading toward the river. Maybe they were going to fish. They didn't have any meat. They were close to the city."

"They must be, if you left home after breakfast, and the sun is still high in the sky." He smiled at me. "Even if you did run all the way back."

Smoke Shell straightened up, suddenly serious and proud. Looking at his broad, copper-colored chest and his flashing black eyes, I thought, not for the first time, that he was the most handsome of all the young men. "Eveningstar Macaw, you were very brave," he said. "Go home now, and do not tell anyone of this. You have done a great thing."

He marched back into the house, gathering around him the gamblers, who had been watching us from the doorway, and calling for the other men of the house. Now that he had taken the responsibility from me, I felt the full exhaustion of the last hour. I trudged slowly down the street to my house. I wasn't worried. My brother was capable of dealing with those Savages.

Feather Dawn sat out front, weaving. "Back so soon?" she asked when she saw me. I ignored her.

I went through our one-room house to the back courtyard. My mother was there, with a few of her patients. I took the rabbit fern out of my bag and laid it beside her.

"Eveningstar! What has happened to you?"

13

"I'm all right," I answered weakly. I was too tired to explain, even if Smoke Shell hadn't forbidden me.

"You're limping."

I hadn't noticed. Mother took off my sandals. Most girls went barefoot, but I needed shoes when I was going into the jungle. Mother looked at my feet and drew a thorn from the right one, near my big toe.

"Why didn't you stop to pull this out?" Mother asked. "And your feet are covered with cuts and blisters." She studied my face a moment, and her sharp features softened. "Never mind, little duck. You look ready to collapse."

She took an ointment from her medicines and rubbed it into my aching feet. The burning began to cool, but I wasn't sure I could stand on them again. Mother lifted me in her arms, leaving my sandals, specked with blood, and carried me inside. She laid me in my bed of thick, woven reed mats and got me some water to drink. I was already sinking into sleep when I felt her kiss on my forehead.

other gently shook me awake at dinner time. She didn't even ask me to get up, just pressed a bowl of steaming stew into my hands. Somewhere she had found some turkey meat, my favorite, to add to the red beans, squash, and peppers. We rarely got meat, except for celebrations, even when times were good. My stomach ached so much with hunger that I couldn't even sit up straight, but I forced myself to eat slowly to savor the rich broth spiced with dried chili peppers. I mopped up the last bit with warm tortillas before settling back with a contented sigh.

"That was the best thing I've ever eaten," I said. "Where did you get turkey?"

"Turkey?" Feather Dawn asked sharply, eyeing my empty bowl and then poking at her dish.

"Sometimes the best medicine is a good meal," my mother said.

Feather Dawn had been throwing me looks throughout dinner, but Mother wouldn't let her ask questions. Finally she could bear no more.

15

"Eveningstar, what happened today?" she burst out. "I want to know!"

"It's all right," I said, almost asleep again. "Smoke Shell will take care of everything."

I slept without dreaming and woke again to the sounds of the grinding stone. Early each morning, my mother would stir up the fire in the hearth and begin to grind corn. She would scoop a handful of yellow and black kernels from the limewater where they had soaked overnight to soften the hulls, and she would spread the corn on top of a rectangular stone with three short legs. Kneeling, she would take a heavy cylinder of the same rough stone and roll it forward and backward across the corn until she had a coarse flour.

The flesh of the first beings, the four mother-fathers, was made from the first of all corn, ground fine by the goddess Ix Chel. When she finished grinding, Ix Chel rinsed her hands, and the fat for the first beings came off of them. Now we get our flesh and our fat from corn, and Mother imitates the goddess every day. I stuck my head into the court-yard, where Mother worked. She saw that I was awake, and smiled.

"Warm tortillas by the hearth, little duck," she said.

I got up, fastened my skirt and shawl, and went into the kitchen building to retrieve a stack of tor-tillas, left over from the night before and recently toasted. I sat on the paving stones next to Mother and watched her mix the ground grain with water to form a thick dough. She put it in a pottery bowl and covered it with cornhusks.

The bowl was a pretty one, the clay painted orange with a design of angular black lines and the figure of a seated jaguar. We didn't usually have such nice pottery, although Father's trade was in ceramics, because he sold the best items. Few could afford real craftsmanship during the war, so my father held on to the nicest pieces and sold bowls and jugs that were unpainted or had simple designs.

When the dough was ready to be made into tortillas for our evening meal, Mother would pat a small lump into a round, flat cake, no thicker than heavy cotton cloth, and bake it on a circular stone griddle placed on the hearth. She'd keep them hot in a gourd until we were ready to eat. My father could eat stacks of them at one meal, and we had them every night, with the leftovers for breakfast, so I wondered if my mother ever got tired of making them. I never got tired of eating them, at least.

When I had finished, I asked what I should look for that day. Mother could see that I was still sore, and perhaps she guessed something about the strangers in the jungle.

"Stay in the city today," she said. "Your sister can teach you to weave."

I nodded with a sigh. My mother had been generous in her statement. It was doubtful whether Feather Dawn or anyone else could ever teach me how to weave anything worth having. I hated weaving and did it terribly. The only good thing about the war was that I no longer had to try to learn, since I was so busy looking for medicine.

But all Mayan women spin and weave cloth for their families and to pay the nobility in tribute and taxes. I would never get a husband without such an essential skill. I tidied my hair, then went out to the courtyard and slumped on the ground next to Feather Dawn.

"Mother says you're to teach me to weave today."

"In one day? Not likely." She was still angry because she didn't know what had happened the day before.

Feather was seated on the ground cross-legged, with her back-strap loom stretched out before her. The loom bar was attached to a post, and long threads connected it to the base bar. Each end of the base bar was attached to an end of the back strap, which went around Feather's waist so that the loom was stretched taut in front of her.

Commoners like us wore cloth made from maguey, yucca, or palm fibers; my own clothes were of light brown palm strands. But Feather Dawn was already good enough to make cotton clothes for the nobles. She dyed the yarn herself with the juice of flowers and

fruits or, when she could get them at the market, with extracts from shellfish or the cochineal, a tiny insect that lives on cactus.

That day she had gray and white threads stretched on the loom in bands of alternating width. She had various shades of blue for the cross strands. Her fingers worked so fast I could barely see them, and I soon got tired of trying.

I looked at the bright balls of yarn and the sewing and weaving tools Feather kept in a long cylindrical reed basket. She had some needles made from cactus spines and others of copper. I pulled out a copper one and tested it against my finger.

"Leave those alone!"

I sighed and replaced the needle.

"What are you making?" I asked.

"A new cloak for Smoke Shell," she grudgingly answered.

The one decent thing about Feather Dawn was that she loved Smoke Shell almost as much as I did. She would rather make him a gift than make something to sell or trade for some trinket she wanted. Or for medicine for people she didn't know.

Feather was beautiful even as a child. She had reddish brown skin, smooth and glossy like wet clay. Her dark, slanting eyes were crossed, and her high forehead was flattened back in a straight line from her long nose.

Perhaps because Feather Dawn was her first daughter, our mother carefully used every trick to enhance her beauty. She bound Feather's head between two boards, front and back, when she was a baby, to flatten her forehead and accentuate the line of her nose. Mother also tied a bead to a strand of hair that hung between Feather's eyes to encourage her to focus inward and develop the crossed eyes that our people find so beautiful. But then, all the mothers do this to their babies; on Feather it just worked better.

I was a restless child and fussed when bound to the cradleboard, Mother said. The only way to keep me quiet and happy was to let me crawl around as I liked, so she had to take the boards off my head early, and the beads were forever disappearing from my hair. Mother thought I used to pull them off and swallow them.

Later, when Feather Dawn turned twelve and became a woman, she pierced her earlobes, her lip, one nostril, and her septum, the flesh between her nostrils, like the older girls. She filed her front teeth to elegant sharp points and began tattooing her body. She wore as much jewelry as she could get, ear plugs, lip plugs, nose rings, arm bands, necklaces, and headbands of onyx, rock crystal, dark red porphyry, mother-of-pearl, copper, and silver. She found some ear plugs made of a green stone that looked almost like jade. The cylinders were large enough to fit over my thickest finger, but the stone was so thin it was transparent. She suffered for weeks until the holes in her earlobes had stretched enough to accommodate these treasures.

Her only desire was to marry a nobleman so she would be allowed to wear gold and jade and to inlay her front teeth with bits of jade. Failing that, she would get Smoke Shell elected to the nobility, so that his family might rise up with him. That was probably one reason Feather made him such wonderful clothes, so that he would look noble and therefore might be thought of as worthy of nobility. But she truly loved him as well.

Feather and I were only a few years old when Smoke Shell had left home at age fourteen to live in a communal house and study warfare and the crafts of men. But he came back to visit often and would swoop me up in his arms when I ran to him and admire whatever Feather Dawn was weaving. Most men are not so kind to their sisters.

On the day I sat watching Feather at her loom, she was a few months short of twelve, with just a little jewelry and simple dresses. But she was already beginning to pile her hair in complicated styles, and older boys were starting to stare at her.

I knew that I would never come near Feather in beauty, grace, or household skills, and so I turned away from such things and said I wasn't interested. I wished I had been born a boy and could join my brother in warfare.

I wondered where Smoke Shell was at that moment. Knowing he must have gone to find the Savages, I amused myself with horrifying daydreams of their battles. Sometimes I imagined that the enemy had captured Smoke Shell and was torturing him viciously, until tears sprang to my eyes and I wanted to rush after him. But I never really believed that any harm could come to him, because he was perfect, and because I loved him.

Later that day I slipped away from Feather Dawn and went by Smoke Shell's house. No one stirred inside. The city seemed not to notice, except for Mother, who mumbled prayers even more often than usual, almost constantly, and Feather Dawn, who grew more agitated and mean in her worry. I seldom saw my father and talked to him even less, so I don't know what he knew. If there were any rumors, he would have heard them in the market, but he would not have told me.

The following day I was allowed to go back to my medicine hunt, so long as I stayed along the edge of the jungle. I went by Smoke Shell's house again in the morning, and still no one was there.

I decided to forage in the direction of the river. Slowly, I ventured farther inward, drawn by curiosity and concern, until I lost my nerve and flew back to the jungle's edge at top speed. All day I repeated this sequence, until at last the sun began to sink and I turned home, my medicine bag nearly empty. At Smoke Shell's house, nothing moved but some scrawny dogs caught in an argument.

Each day passed the same. The farmers had begun to plant, poking holes in the ground with chest-high digging sticks, then reaching into sacks for a few kernels of corn, or perhaps some beans or squash seeds, and dropping them inside the hole. They kicked dirt over the hole, took a step, and repeated the process. They were at work by the time I headed into the jungle, and when I came home they were still at work, stopping only occasionally for a drink of cornmeal and water from a gourd.

After several days had passed, I came out of the jungle one afternoon to rest a little and eat a few tortillas Mother had given me, and I saw that the fields were empty.

I knew something wonderful or terrible must have happened, so I rushed into the city, past empty houses, until I reached the city center, where the religious and public buildings are. I heard a great noise ahead and saw a few stragglers like myself hurrying toward it.

I could not see over the crowd clogging the central plaza, so I pushed through them. The people jostled and crushed together, their bright cloaks and headdresses swaying in a tangle of color. I was small and used to squeezing through tight spots among the jungle vines, so I soon made my way to the front, where I could see men standing on the steps of the Temple of the First Oracle.

The warriors were back, even more victorious than in my greatest fantasies. Most of the original party had returned, Smoke Shell among them. Their copper breastplates gleamed in the sun, and copper, silver, or polished stone glinted at their ears and noses. The red, black, and white war paint on their faces and bodies was fresh; they must have renewed it before returning to the city. With their arms and lower legs covered with tattoos, they were frightening and glorious. Headdresses of bright macaw feathers held back their long, glossy black hair. They carried their rolled-up shields and their flint knives at their waists and held obsidian-tipped spears in their hands. They looked like young gods, standing proudly on the temple steps in the sun.

On the lowest steps, a group of captives huddled. Some shrank back, frightened and miserable, while a few stood defiant but powerless. I saw Small, looking wretched. Their arms were bound behind their backs at the elbows. They had, of course, been stripped of their weapons, but made to carry their other belongings and those they had stolen. Most had wounds, but they had not been starved or mistreated after their capture. To have healthy, strong captives would make the warriors look even greater and would make a better sacrifice to the gods.

The warriors were joined by several lords, men of noble family picked by the king to oversee the government and act as judges. Smoke Shell stepped forward, and the crowd quieted. He greeted the lords in a ringing voice, so all could hear.

"We have made war with the Savages. We have killed many and captured these here. We give them to our beloved King Flint Sky God and to the gods in sacrifice. They will bother our villages no more."

The crowd roared, and the lords bowed to the young warriors. Smoke Shell saw me watching from the front of the crowd. He came to me, holding out his hand, and I rushed to him. He lifted me in his arms, shouting, "Here is the child who saved us. She saw the Savages in the jungle and told me where to find them. Give thanks to Eveningstar Macaw."

The people cheered some more, but I was distracted by the group of captives. Small saw me and started to smile with surprise. But the smile faded as he studied Smoke Shell and me. I felt sorry for Small as I realized that he had betrayed his people through his kindness to me.

"That one there," I said, pointing to Small. "He saw me in the jungle, and he let me go. I don't want him to die."

Smoke Shell scrutinized Small, then called over a lord.

"This one showed generosity to my sister, and because of it we found him and destroyed our enemy. I would keep him from the sacrifice and make him a slave."

The lord studied us all for a moment.

"As you wish."

CHAPTER THREE

That evening was a great celebration. People killed their last ducks and turkeys and all but their best dogs for the feast.

A group of musicians snaked through the crowd. Several men kept a rhythm by shaking copper bells or rattles made of clay, metal, gourds, or strings of large seeds. Others blew trumpets and whistles or played clay flutes decorated with figures of people or animals. Dancers clad in jaguar-skin pants, gloves, and headdresses spun and stomped amid clouds of fragrant black smoke from the burning balls of copal resin. Masked actors and clowns performed plays, and storytellers recited our oldest legends. With so much to see, it all blurred together in one overwhelming impression of pageantry.

In gracious thanks to the gods, people gave sacrifices of food, animals, and ornaments. The captives would be saved for a later sacrifice, after the proper period of fasting and purification rites.

We also fed the gods through a bloodletting ritual

that night. All the people except the youngest children and some of the foreign slaves were making this greatest act of homage, drawing thorns or stingray spines through their ears, nostrils, lips, tongues, or other body parts until the blood flowed. I saw my mother bandaging the arm of a man who had cut himself too deeply, while nearby a woman slumped against a wall, her eyes rolling back in her head, faint from loss of blood and from alcohol.

Smoke Shell led me into the temple of Yam Kax, the young corn god. With Smoke Shell to guide me, I took a long, sharp stingray spine and held it to my earlobe, steadying the tip of the lobe with my other hand. Then I pressed it through with a quick shove. After a sharp moment of pain, which made my eyes open wide, I felt an intense throbbing, but no worse than many injuries I had gotten in the jungle or when playing too roughly around home.

"Now pull it through the other side," Smoke Shell told me.

I did as he said, slowly drawing the slender spine out the back of my ear. It was a tingly sort of pain that made me want to shiver.

"Now open your eyes," Smoke Shell said.

I didn't remember closing them, but my eyelids were pressed tight into my face. I relaxed and looked at my brother crouched in front of me, smiling.

"Brave little one. You would make a good warrior."

He stood up quickly, drawing a slender, needle-sharp obsidian knife.

He lifted his head, stuck out his tongue, and plunged the knife into his tongue.

Bright drops of red splattered his neck and chest. He drew the knife out, and a stream of blood ran down his chin and spotted the ground.

He watched me, his eyes flashing with humor. He held out the knife, sticky with his blood, in the open palm of his hand. I stared at it, unable to move.

Smoke Shell laughed. "Next time, little one."

The sun slid out of sight behind the temples, and soon the sky was black except for the multitude of flashing stars and a distant crescent moon. Torches cast long dancing shadows, and the masked perform-ers looked like wild demons in the yellow glow. The adults drank deep gourds of balché, a liquor made from corn, and their steps grew unsteady.

A lord came with a message for Smoke Shell and me. King Flint Sky God wanted to see us.

The lord, an old man named Frog Boar, led us to the royal palace. As we walked up the steps to the main entrance, I leaned close to Smoke Shell. He rested his hand lightly on my shoulder.

At the top of the temple steps, the high priest, Great Skull Zero, met us, and Frog Boar retreated. Great Skull Zero was a tall man, a head taller than most of the village men and more than two heads taller than me. He was heavy, too, with rolls of fat at his waist, and no wonder, as he got all the best food, and meat every day. He stared at Smoke Shell, his flabby face hardening into a frown, but my brother was too excited to notice. Then Great Skull Zero looked at me, his black eyes boring into me with no hint of kindness, and I shuddered at the power in them.

We passed through a short corridor and stepped into the throne room, lit by torches in wall sconces. King Flint Sky God sat cross-legged on a stone platform covered with jaguar skins. A guard on either side of him held one edge of an embroidered linen cloth in front of the god-king's face, so that no one could talk directly to him. He was richly attired in a tunic covered with brilliant green quetzal feathers, a matching headdress, a necklace of polished jade beads so big I could not have fit two of them in my hand, and gold and jade arm bands and anklets.

I peeked out from behind Smoke Shell's shoulder, suddenly shy and afraid.

"Come closer, child."

The voice from behind the cloth was thin and dry, an old man's voice. I stepped forward and sat on the floor, and I heard a rustle as Smoke Shell sat just behind me. My eyes were level with the king's knees, and I stared at his sandals covered with jade beads. I noticed that his ankles were thin and bumpy and the hair on his legs was white against his brown skin. Very few Maya live long enough for any of their hair to go white, but this was a god-king.

"You saw the foreign Savages in the jungle."

I nodded, still looking down.

"What were you doing, alone in the jungle?"

"Gathering medicine for my mother."

"Ah, yes. I know your mother's work. Blue Quetzal is an excellent healer."

I was surprised that a king would know of my mother. I straightened up, swelled with pride.

"When you saw these men," the king said, "why did you tell only your brother?"

"Who else would I have told?" I asked, confused.

He laughed, gently. "I hope you have as much faith in your gods as you do in this young warrior, child. Smoke Shell."

My brother edged forward and bowed his head before our king.

"Your Majesty."

"How is it that you have done what our entire army has not been able to do?"

Smoke Shell looked up, his eyes shining as he recounted the tale. "I got all the warriors in my house and we went into the jungle as soon as we heard the news. We found the group Eveningstar saw. They were fishing in the foothills just above the farmland. We surprised them. We killed them easily. Then, when we were cleaning up in the river, another one came back. The boy who saw her earlier and let her go."

Small had left the group for a while, perhaps to avoid their anger. He had come back when the battle was over, walking into a clearing to find his companions dead and enemy warriors waiting.

Smoke Shell continued, gesturing excitedly with his strong hands. "He ran off, and I held the warriors back. We could have captured that boy right away, but I wanted to know what he would do. We tracked him through the jungle, one of us creeping close behind him while the others followed at a distance.

"We followed all night and the next day. He led us to a larger group of Savages. I got down on my stomach so I could creep close and watch them. They were all excited; they picked up their weapons and shouted a lot. But it was nearly dark, so finally they went to sleep."

Usually the warriors declare a truce each night until the following morning. But usually the fighting is out in the open and both sides are warned far in advance. The Savages had not followed our rules of warfare, so Smoke Shell followed theirs.

"When they were all asleep, I went back to the rest of my group. We surrounded the camp and attacked suddenly and silently. We each killed at least one before they woke up. I was killing my third before he had time to yell. There were still more of them than us, but we surprised them. We killed the rest or disabled them."

Smoke Shell set his shoulders back proudly. "We lost only three Mayan warriors. They were good men. We brought back the bodies for proper burial."

Great Skull Zero stepped forward. I had forgotten that he was waiting behind us. The high priest scowled at Smoke Shell.

"When you heard of these Savages, why did you not tell the war captain and the other warriors?"

His voice was stern, and I worried that Smoke Shell was in trouble. My brother opened his mouth and then hesitated, looking concerned for the first time that evening. He turned back to the king.

"Your Majesty," Smoke Shell said slowly, "for two years we have tried to fight the Savages with our entire army. It did not work. We take too long to prepare and too long to get to the enemy, and we make too much noise as we approach. Our usual form of warfare, with elaborate ceremonies and attendants blowing trumpets and waving brightly feathered banners, does not work against the Savages. We know this from unfortunate experience."

"Yes, go on."

"With a small group, we were able to leave within an hour of hearing the news. We could move quietly, so that we gave no warning of our approach. We could cover great distances quickly, finding enough food on the way to feed our small group, so we were not slowed by carrying a week's worth of meals on our backs. I am sorry if I offended Your Majesty or the war captain by acting without approval."

Smoke Shell stared straight ahead, his face and shoulders tight. I thought wildly for something I could say to save my brother.

"You were right, of course," the king said. "The other soldiers are disappointed about missing the action and angry about missing the glory. But you have saved our people. Rise, Smoke Shell."

Smoke Shell rose, smiling with relief.

King Flint Sky God continued. "You have proven yourself brave and worthy. I now appoint you a lord."

Smoke Shell's relief blossomed into a joy that transformed his face.

The high priest interrupted. "He must not be allowed to go without punishment. He has disobeyed our rules. I should have been informed before this battle. You must not reward him for this insult."

The king answered him gently. "My honorable friend, you know I could not rule this city without you. But we will need new help in the years ahead. I believe this young man will be of great use to us."

He turned back to Smoke Shell. "But the high priest is right. The greatest glory comes from obedience, to the gods and to your city. I trust you will not make such a mistake again."

Smoke Shell bowed his head and spoke softly. "I'm sorry. I didn't . . ." He took a deep breath and looked up, his features hardening. "I promise, Your Majesty. I will dedicate my life to obedience. Whether I am a warrior, a lord, or a farmer, I will follow orders. I will not make this mistake again."

"I would like you to study under the interpreters," the king said. "You will study astronomy, mathematics, writing, and the calendar. The discipline will be good for you. You will have many opportunities to advance yourself. Your family is full of courage and intelligence. You are all noble from this day forth."

nd so we joined the nobility. King Flint Sky God gave Smoke Shell presents of gold and jade. We received land in the noble area, and we built a stone house, set up on a platform like the other noble houses. Normally the courtyard, kitchen building, garden, and cement cistern for water storage would have been surrounded by other houses from our family group. We had only our own small family, so we built a stone wall to enclose our plaza. When Feather Dawn and I married, we would tear down sections of the wall and build new houses for ourselves, our husbands, and the children we would someday bear.

We had a leaving ceremony for our old wood-and-thatch home. A priest sacrificed a turkey to honor our ancestors who lay buried beneath the courtyard. The priest, Smoking Squirrel, was an old family friend and my mother's cousin. As I watched him sprinkle blood over the foundations, I thought of my aunt and cousins buried there and the grandparents and great-grandparents I had never known.

We had a great feast, then smashed the dishes we'd used and scattered the pieces over our old home, along with bits of jade we crushed with rocks. Then we said good-bye and moved to our new house and to our new status in the upper level of society.

We moved just before the sacrifice of the Savages and the sacred ball game that accompanied it. We Maya sacrifice people only in times of crisis or for special ceremonies. The sun, rain, and earth gods must be fed by human blood in order to keep the cosmic order, but usually bloodletting ceremonies are enough.

We had important foreign warriors to sacrifice this time, and the ritual would not only symbolize our victory, but feed and honor the gods so they might return us to the peace and prosperity we had once known.

On the day of the sacrifice, people flooded the ballcourt arena. Because of Smoke Shell's new honor, we joined the top lords and priests on the platform that interrupted the temple stairs just a few steps down from the top plaza. The temple overlooked the court. Lesser nobles, merchants, and professionals sat toward the bottom of the steps or on the sloped side walls of the court, looking down into a rectangular playing field, which had a crossbar at each end. Everyone wore their best clothes, colorful cloaks, and feathered headdresses, with jewelry glinting everywhere. The rows of people looked like strings of brightly polished precious stones lying in tangled, shimmering masses.

We also got a close view of the rituals that accompanied the sacred game and sacrifice. I sat with Smoking Squirrel, who was an interpreter. The interpreters were the class of priests that told the future, appointed holy days, treated the sick, and taught the sciences. Smoking Squirrel was not only my mother's cousin and friend, but now he was also Smoke Shell's teacher.

Smoking Squirrel was a kind man, older than my mother but not as tough. His broad back was crooked from a serious illness he'd had as a child, and his smile was crooked, too, but in a nice, friendly way, as if he were seeing the good and bad in everything, and the good was just winning. He wore a macaw-feather ornament in his nose, the base of the feather shaft piercing his septum and the dusky red feather curving out longer than my forearm and fading to blue at the tip. It bobbed when he laughed or nodded, and when he turned quickly it brushed my face. While we waited for the sacrifice to begin, he told me the story of the Hero Twins.

"It all began with a pair of twins, One Marksman and Seven Marksman," Smoking Squirrel explained. "They were not the Hero Twins," he added, leaning closer. "We'll get to them in a bit. One Marksman and Seven Marksman made too much noise playing the ball game and angered the Lords of Death who lived below the ball court. The brothers were called to the underworld, tricked by the Lords of Death, and sacrificed.

"The Lords of Death buried One Marksman under the ball court. They hung the skull of Seven Marksman in a gourd tree to warn others not to offend the gods of the underworld. But Blood Moon, a daughter of one of the Lords of Death, found the skull," Smoking Squirrel said. "It spit into her hand, and she became pregnant. Her father was furious, so the girl escaped to the middleworld, where the grandmother of the dead twins took care of her.

"Blood Moon gave birth to twins, Venus Lord and First Jaguar. Intelligent and courageous, the brothers had many adventures. Then they found the ball-game gear of their father and uncle. They became expert ball players, but they, too, disturbed the Lords of Death. Venus Lord and First Jaguar were called to the underworld, the place of fear, and given a series of challenges. If they failed any one, they would die.

"The first night, the twins were put in the Dark House." Smoking Squirrel said the name in a low voice that made me shudder. "For their test, they had to keep a torch and two cigars lit all through the long night. It was impossible! The fires burned out long before dawn, but the twins put fireflies at the tips of the cigars and pretended a bright red macaw feather was the light of the torch. When the Lords of Death peeked in the window, they were fooled.

"In the morning, the twins challenged the Lords of Death to a ball game. They agreed on a bet: the losers had to give the winners four bowls of flowers by the next morning. The twins were better players, but they allowed themselves to lose.

"The Lords of Death made it difficult for the brothers to pay their bet. They liked a challenge," Smoking Squirrel said. "They put the twins in Razor House, where stone blades moved by themselves, searching for something to cut. 'We'll bring you animal flesh,' the twins promised. 'Much better than ours.' So the stones stopped moving. Then the twins asked leaf-cutting ants to bring back flowers. The ants did the brothers' bidding and found beautiful flowers for the twins. In the morning, the Lords of Death were furious when they found that the twins had paid them with flowers from the lords' own gardens.

"Every day the twins played ball with the lords, and every night they endured another test. They conquered the freezing wind and hail of Cold House, the hungry cats of Jaguar House, and the flames of Fire House.

"They escaped the shrieking bats of Bat House by hiding in their blowguns. When the bats grew quiet in the morning, Venus Lord poked his head out, thinking all was safe. A giant bat flew at him and knocked off his head, sending it rolling into the ball court.

"First Jaguar thought quickly. He carved a squash to look like Venus Lord's head and placed it upon his brother's shoulders. The twins went once more to play the Lords of Death, who used Venus Lord's head as a ball. First Jaguar kicked the head into the tall grass alongside the court. A rabbit hiding there bounded off like a ball, and the lords followed.

"First Jaguar grabbed his brother's head and replaced it on Venus Lord's body, setting the squash in the grass. He called to the lords, and the game resumed with the squash as a ball. But when a lord tried to knock the ball with his hip, the squash splattered all over the ball court and the lords.

"The lords were so angry they decided to burn the twins to death. When they heard of their fate, the brothers asked two seers to give the lords certain instructions for disposing of their remains.

"The lords, thinking themselves clever and subtle, invited the twins to see the huge stone fire pit they used to brew alcohol. 'How about a little contest?' one lord said. 'I'll bet you can't jump over that flaming pit.' The twins wasted no time; they simply jumped into the flames and died.

"'We have won!' the Lords of Death shouted, laughing together. Then they did as the seers suggested, grinding the twins' bones to dust and tossing the powder into the river. Five days later, First Jaguar and Venus Lord were resurrected—but they had the faces of catfish! The next day, they returned to fully human form.

"The twins dressed like wandering actors. They traveled, performing miracle dances. The Lords of Death heard about the marvelous performances and asked the actors to come to their court. They never suspected they were inviting the Hero Twins.

"The disguised twins performed a startling dance for the lords—First Jaguar dismembered Venus Lord and then brought him back to life. The Lords of Death were very much impressed. 'Let us join the dance,' they begged.

"The twins agreed. They killed and dismembered them—but did not resurrect them. The Hero Twins had outsmarted death. Venus Lord rose as Sun, and when Sun went down, First Jaguar rose on the other side of the world as Full Moon. Now, people have hope that when they die, they, too, will be able to conquer death and become honored ancestors like the Hero Twins."

When Smoking Squirrel finished this story, he sat back on the temple steps and smiled at me, the smile reaching both sides of his face evenly for once.

"So you see, child, why the ball game is such an important ceremony. We reenact the Hero Twins' defeat of the Lords of Death."

I nodded. "I would have liked to see those miracle dances," I said. I licked moisture off my lips and glanced at the sky with surprise. Rain was falling in a gentle drizzle.

"You'll see something like it during the sacrifice. Only no one will return to life here, and I suppose that would be the most impressive part. But the important thing to remember is that the Hero Twins won not through force of strength, but by outwitting their opponents."

"Smoke Shell did the same thing."

"Yes. Now, are you as clever as your brother?" he asked with a teasing smile that prevented me from being embarrassed.

"I sometimes act before I think."

"Ah. Sometimes one must decide quickly, when taking the time to sort through all the evidence and options will cause the best of those options to slip away. But you must be careful, or you will cause yourself a great deal of trouble someday."

"Probably." I studied the flat jade pendant that lay against his bare chest, light green like a new leaf, and picked out the two-headed reptile that represented the god Itzamna among the carved figures. "Feather Dawn says I have no sense."

"You are young. You follow Ix Chel, like your mother, don't you?"

"Of course." Ix Chel, the moon goddess, was

patroness of medicine and weaving, the goddess of women and childbirth.

"Yes, Lady Moon is strong in your family, with your mother's medicine and your sister's weaving. Have you considered becoming a priestess?"

I was startled. Now that I belonged to a noble family, I could join a religious order. I was flattered that Smoking Squirrel thought I would be a suitable priestess, but I knew that girls only took care of the temple, sweeping the floors and tending the sacred fires. I was used to more freedom, and much more excitement.

"I want to be a healer like Mother."

He sighed. "Yes, that is probably a better choice for you. I would like to see more girls with real intelligence and courage in the temples, but I suppose there wouldn't be much chance for you to use those qualities. You will continue to serve Ix Chel faithfully in your own way, I hope. Service to the gods is the greatest thing we can do in life."

"Even greater than winning the war with the Savages?" I asked, teasing him now.

He smiled, but spoke seriously. "If destroying our enemy were all that we cared about, the warriors could have killed all the Savages when they found them. That would have been simpler and safer than taking captives."

"Bringing back captives took more courage and brought them more honor."

"Yes, but why? So we can feed the gods with the captives' blood, bringing the world into balance with our sacrifice. Smoke Shell earned honor by honoring the gods."

"I guess it's like the bloodletting ceremony," I said slowly. "It takes courage to do it, but that isn't why we do it. We draw our blood to honor the gods and feed them."

"Yes. When one forgets the gods, and acts only for his own glory, then the world is put out of balance. But look, the game is about to begin."

We turned toward the two doorways at the top of the temple as silence fell over the crowd, starting with the lords and traveling down through the commoners. Smoking Squirrel hurried to take his place among the priests, and they began a rhythmic chant.

I gasped as the first figure came out of the temple through a cloud of incense smoke and misty rain. I knew it must be King Flint Sky God, but with his deep green jade mask and the shimmering green quetzal feathers billowing up from his elaborate head-dress, he truly looked like a god from the upperworld who had magically materialized on earth. His jade breastplate was carved with the face of a jaguar god, and he held a ceremonial war club of gleaming gold.

The ball-game players followed behind him. Our Mayan team marched out, the first two dressed in the costumes of the Hero Twins—First Jaguar with patches of jaguar pelt on his chin, arms, and legs, and Venus Lord with large dots on his cheek, arms, and legs. The captives followed, dressed as the Lords of Death and guarded on each side by warriors. Both teams looked proud and fierce, but only our side looked excited.

The king stepped aside at the top of the stairs, and the athletes descended into the ball court. The crowd cheered, and I with them, until the men reached their positions and the game began.

Our team started with the ball, which was as big as my head and made of hard, solid rubber. The leader tossed the ball up and then bounced it off the thick protective pad he wore around his hips. The ball hit the sloped stone wall on the side of the court and spun back. Another player dove and managed to deflect the ball off his arm pad.

Both teams struggled to keep the ball from hitting the ground and risk angering the Lords of Death beneath. They could use arms, knees, or hips, but no hands or feet. The court was large, so the players really had to struggle to get to one end. Our team was making some headway, though, blocking the Savages whenever they got control of the ball and slowly forcing them back.

Finally, the Maya dressed as First Jaguar took a massive swing at the ball with his arm and sent it flying toward the opposition. A Savage threw up his arm to block but slipped on the wet stone and landed on the ground. The ball sailed out the open end of the court past the stone marker. We had scored!

The crowd roared its approval, and the Mayan team strutted back to center court, the Savages trailing behind.

Clearly the Savages had played this game before, or one similar, but they were probably not the best players from their tribe, and they didn't have the support of the crowd and the comfort of a familiar court. Still, they fought hard and won the respect of most of those who watched them. The Maya love nothing so much as a good ball game.

When the game was over, the players straightened their damp, rumpled costumes, brushed off some of the dirt, and assembled at the base of the temple steps, warm and tired but still proud.

The game ended in a tie, as most ball games do. The scoring is arranged so that these games seldom have clear winners. If a team does win, they have the right to take whatever clothes and jewelry the spectators are wearing—if they can catch them.

We had no such excitement for this game, but by the end I was exhilarated and would gladly have given my jewelry for the privilege of watching.

The king descended the temple steps and spoke to the two teams.

"Excellent game! Both sides played with courage,

and you have tied. Because the foreign team played well, their lives will be spared and they will become slaves. Only those captives who could not play will be sacrificed."

The Savages stood close together, warily watching the king and the warriors nearby. They did not look happy about their reprieve. Then I realized that they probably could not speak Mayan. They still didn't know what would happen to them.

Warriors led the Savages to the bottom of the steps, where they would see the sacrifice. The Mayan athletes were invited up the temple to watch. The game had been exciting, but the real ceremony was just beginning.

he events that followed seemed like a dream, a strange, fascinating, horrible fever dream one gets when very sick and sleep is shallow and troubled by hallucinations. I'd seen sacrifices before, but always from far off in the plaza. They seemed like shows, extravagant pageants, part of the singing and dancing and storytelling that fill every major celebration.

This time I was watching from the temple itself, close enough to see the faces of the victims. And they were not warriors captured in a battle I knew nothing about or orphans bought from another city. These people were there, in part, because of me.

The eight captives who were to be sacrificed were brought out of the temple, each with an armed guard at his elbow. The Savages' bodies were painted blue, the color of sacrifice, and they wore white loincloths. A few had whatever ornaments they had been wearing when captured—leather bracelets, necklaces of silver and copper, or feathered headdresses—so the viewers and the gods would know that these were not just poor men, but warriors and leaders of their tribe. Most of this group had been badly injured in the battle, and one had even lost an arm, but they had been doctored and well fed in their captivity. They were able to stand tall and defiant, but most of their faces betrayed fear, or anger, or both.

Small was not among them, of course, because he was now our slave. When I remembered him, I looked around and saw him huddled in a ball, pressed against the low wall alongside the temple steps, with his face against his knees and his arms covering his head. I realized how young he was, barely old enough to be a warrior. My heart wrenched with guilt and pity. I went over to him and laid a hand tentatively on his shoulder. He raised his head slightly to look at me, the muscles in his face tight around his red-rimmed eyes.

"It's all right," I said. "Those who are sacrificed go straight to the gods."

He stared at me, his expression unchanging. He couldn't understand me. He had not yet learned more than a few words of our language. On an impulse, I put my arms around him in a quick hug, the only way I could think of to offer some sympathy. I supposed he had every right to pull away, but he just gave me a small, weak smile and buried his head in his arms again.

The king started to talk, so I turned back to watch

the ceremony. My thoughts were still distracted by Small, and I had a hard time paying attention as first King Flint Sky God and then the high priest, Great Skull Zero, spoke and prayed before the crowd. The sun beat down, and I felt dizzy and thirsty. I watched the captives and wondered what it felt like to know that you would soon be dead.

Finally the sacrifice itself began. Four guards dressed in rich costumes grabbed one of the captives and dragged him forward. Perhaps the suddenness of their actions startled him; for whatever reason, he began to struggle, although he must have known it was useless. The guards forced him back over a low stone altar and each held one of his arms or legs as he squirmed and babbled in his strange language.

Great Skull Zero stepped forward holding a knife as long as my forearm. The black stone gleamed in the sunlight as the high priest lifted the blade high above his head. His murmuring prayers rose in volume to a roar, and he plunged the knife into the victim's chest. The Savage squealed and thrashed one last time and then lay still.

The crowd below roared, their voices raised in praise of the gods. My voice joined the words automatically, but my eyes went from the body of the first victim, blood gushing from his chest, to the faces of the remaining Savages. Some stared in horror at their comrade, or perhaps the horror was at their own fate.

Some refused to look, their eyes closed or turned to the sky as they whispered prayers.

The dead man was bound into the shape of a ball. Great Skull Zero stepped aside for King Flint Sky God, who gave the body a mighty push and sent it bouncing down the temple steps, past my family and the other watching nobles and down to the base where the Savages who had played the ball game stood, finally coming to a stop among the crowd in the courtyard.

The next victim was brought forward, and despite what he had just witnessed, he went quietly. He neither struggled nor screamed, dying bravely and honorably. His body, too, was bound and sent spinning down the steps. This part of the ritual reflected the ball game, only now the ball was a human body.

The remaining six victims followed, some dying quietly, some with prayers or tears. Their deaths blurred together for me, much as their blood blended together in a pool around the altar.

Finally the sacrifice was over. Mother touched my shoulder and handed me a gourd of water, which I drank with relief. She did not comment on what we had just witnessed. When I had enough, she took the gourd to Small, still huddled against the wall, and made him drink some.

I looked for the other Savages, the living ones, at the base of the temple steps. They were being led away and would be divided up as slaves among the highest ranking families.

For the rest of us, the day was far from over. We had fed the gods with the blood of the sacrificial victims. Now we would offer them our own.

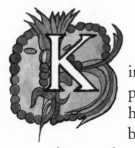

ing Flint Sky God retreated into the temple to prepare for his bloodletting, while
healers and priests began to pray and offer
blessings. Lower priests brought out
incense burners, drum-shaped clay stands depicting
the masks of the Hero Twins, placing them among us
on the temple platforms and down in the plaza.

Soft murmurs drifted from the crowd while I studied the paintings alongside the two temple doorways.
To the left was a scene of great dignitaries in ceremonial clothes, led by a young King Flint Sky God with
the wife and children who all had died some years
before. Dancers nearby were putting on costumes
decorated with quetzal feathers, and on a lower panel
actors wearing earth-god masks were surrounded by
musicians with drums, rattles, and trumpets.

Between the two doorways was a scene of warfare.
Warriors attacked their opponents, while to one side
the prisoners, stripped down to their loincloths, knelt
before our victorious lords in submission.

To the right of the doorways the mural depicted the

final scene in this history. The king, his family, and the important lords whirled in swirls of color, dancing in a frenzy of ecstasy. In the center of the scene, attendants held a dead captive by his hands and feet, while nobles in floor-length white capes watched.

Those scenes, which must have occurred years before I was born, were startlingly like the present. The recent battle had been carried out with less fanfare, but the victory and celebration shown on the walls were as familiar to me as if I had personally witnessed them.

I wondered what monuments would be built to this recent war and if Smoke Shell's name would appear on them. Would future generations remember my brother's great deed? Would I bring my children to a temple such as this one to tell them the story of our victory over the Savages and my own small part in it?

I started from my reverie with the realization that the crowd was silent. King Flint Sky God stood in the temple doorway. His long graying hair was tied atop his head with a plume of feathers that trailed down his back. A strand of jade beads hung around his neck, and below it a carved rectangle of deep green jade as big as both my hands together was suspended on a leather thong. Blue-green strands of jade covered his wrists, ankles, and knees, and a feather ornament pierced the septum of his nose. For clothing he wore only a blindingly white loincloth.

The king slowly and solemnly walked to the top of the temple steps, where he was visible to the crowds below. He stood as proud as a young man, although I knew he had been fasting for days and must have been weak. In years past, his wife and sons would have preceded him in the bloodletting ceremony, but now he was the only living member of his royal family.

Great Skull Zero went to the king's side. He was dressed in a floor-length white cloak like those pictured in the third mural, and he held a shallow bowl filled with fresh, light tan strips of beaten-bark paper, a rope, and a stingray spine. The high priest took the thin, sharp spine and held it above his head. King Flint Sky God closed his eyes and stuck his tongue out as far as it would go. With a swift, practiced slash, the high priest drove the stingray spine through the king's tongue.

King Flint Sky God did not flinch or utter a sound. He calmly took the rope, which was as thick as his finger, and threaded it through the wound in his tongue as the blood poured down his chin and into the bowl the high priest held to the king's chest.

The high priest took some of the blood-soaked paper from the bowl and dropped it into the knee-high incense burner at their feet, along with offerings of corn kernels, rubber, and incense made from resin of the copal tree. The resin caught fire, and the Smoke of the Blood of Trees began to rise.

The king pulled the end of the rope through his tongue and dropped it into the bowl, swaying as a trance overtook him. He danced with blood pouring down his chest and staining his white loincloth. The king's legs gave way and he fell back, sitting on his right hip as black smoke billowed from the burning paper, forming a writhing column around him.

The deep, wailing moan of a conch-shell trumpet sounded the arrival of the Vision Serpent. A roar of praise and awe swept the crowd at the sight of the smoke rising as the double-headed serpent. The king had become the World Tree, materializing the center of the world here at the temple and opening a door to the otherworld. The Vision Serpent's throat formed the path for the gods and ancestral dead to commune with the king.

Around me, flint blades and stingray spines flashed as people slashed their arms and ears, drawing blood from their own bodies as an offering to the god before them. Reminded of my duty, I drew a small dagger from my waistband and pierced my ear. As the warm blood dribbled down my neck, I was caught in the ecstatic frenzy of those around me and began dancing wildly with them, whirling as the trumpets and drums rose in crashing waves of sound.

We let the blood soak into cloth bands tied to our wrists and arms, then dropped the bands into smoking incense burners set among us, calling forth our own ancestors through the door to the otherworld opened by King Flint Sky God.

When the Vision Serpent finally began to fade, and the smoke from the king's incense burner trailed off in gray swirls, Great Skull Zero bent next to King Flint Sky God and helped him to stand. The high priest supported the king with his arm and led him back into the temple.

The music lost its frenzy and softened into a gentle rhythm. We slowed our dancing, and finally stopped, swaying from the power of our joy and faint from the lost blood that splattered our clothing and the stone below our feet in crimson drops.

I noticed the sun hovering low on the horizon and was startled that so much time had passed. But at the same time, so much had happened that it seemed impossible to fit everything into a single day. Suddenly exhausted and hungry, I found my mother and sat at her feet. She handed me a gourd and I drank the last of the cornmeal thinned with water, now warm and too thick from the sun and the dancing.

e weren't used to being noble, and I think Feather Dawn was the only one who enjoyed it wholeheartedly from the start. People kept coming to visit us, which made her feel important but annoyed the rest of us. We always had to be dressed nicely and have good food available and be ready to smile and make small talk at a moment's notice.

Mother said most of them were just curious about us and wanted to be known as friends of the great Smoke Shell and his family. We could even get away with being a little eccentric, since after all Smoke Shell had succeeded by not following the rules, but if we were too different, people would think that we didn't deserve to be noble, and they might ostracize us.

As if all that weren't enough, we were expected to give a feast soon. My father grumbled about the cost, Mother said that she had more important things to do, and I dreaded the idea of getting all dressed up and being watched by hundreds of people I barely knew. Feather Dawn thought we should do it as soon as possible.

Small lived with us, of course, and he was an excellent servant. He was polite and he worked hard, even harder than we asked. Mother simply couldn't find that much for him to do, though, so she and I were teaching him Mayan. He learned quickly, although he remained distant and quiet.

Whenever we went to the market, we took Small with us to help carry back goods. If we passed other Savage slaves, they would scowl at him and usually say something in their language that sounded, from the way they said it, like curses or insults. The owners of the other slaves would sometimes hit them for talking in their own language, but that didn't stop them.

When people came to visit us, they sometimes brought these slaves. It was considered a mark of prestige to have one of the Savages. They weren't even very good servants, except for Small. Since they didn't speak Mayan, they couldn't follow orders well. Most of their owners seemed to forget that. They called the Savages stupid, lazy, or insolent and punished them with beatings, or by tossing chili peppers in a fire and making the slaves lean over the smoke until their eyes burned.

Small seemed nervous all the time. He didn't like to be far from us. I was beginning to feel nervous myself, although I didn't know why.

A few weeks after the ball game, a woman named Three Deer visited, bringing her two daughters, her Savage, and three Mayan slaves. The Savage spoke to Small in a low, angry voice. Small seemed afraid, and when he answered, his voice was pleading. Mother saw all this with watchful eyes, but she didn't say anything so neither did I. But Three Deer was furious. She grabbed a stick she had brought with her and began to hit the Savage on the head and shoulders, screaming at him to be quiet. Mother yelled at her to stop. Finally she had to pull Three Deer away.

Three Deer swung to face Mother with squinting eyes as her chest heaved and her little mouth twisted. Then she stomped out of the house. Her daughters quietly got up to follow, and the Mayan slaves helped the Savage to walk.

Mother watched them leave, then sighed and turned back to us. "The courtyard needs to be cleaned," she said.

Feather Dawn hopped up. "I need to go to the market for some yarn," she said, dashing out of the house.

Mother smiled and motioned for Small and me to follow her. She sat us down in the courtyard, which was perfectly clean, and spoke to Small solemnly.

"You're afraid of the other people in your tribe."

"Yes. They mad. I make warriors to come."

"It wasn't your fault. You were tricked."

"Yes, my fault. Is better I die."

"But you didn't die," Mother scolded him, "so the gods must have wanted you to live."

"They kill me." At first I thought he meant the gods would, but he was talking about the other Savages.

"Have they said they will kill you?"

"Yes." He fidgeted and looked away, refusing to meet our eyes.

"Small," Mother said, forcing him to look at her with her tone of voice, "there is something more. Tell us."

"I no betray them more time," he said desperately.

"You won't betray them. I promise. I promise to the goddess Ix Chel and I promise to you. We want to help."

He stared at her for a long time, searching her face and no doubt wondering if he could trust us. I held my breath and sat quietly. Finally Small let all his breath out in a whoosh and then began to talk.

"They make, they make betray," he said, his Mayan even worse in the rush to get it all out now. "Bad. Go home. Maybe kill."

Mother thought for a moment. "You mean that they're planning to escape, and they may kill some people when they do it?"

"Yes. Escape. Kill family and leave night."

"They told you this?"

He took a deep breath and spoke slowly, searching for the right words. "They say, 'When we escape, we kill you. You and . . .'" He trailed off and looked at me, then away. "They kill me, yes, but you no bad. Bad to kill many people."

"This is serious," Mother said. She spoke calmly, but my heart was pounding. People wanted to kill me! I looked around nervously, as if they might burst in at any moment.

"We must tell Smoke Shell," I exclaimed. "He'll know what to do."

"No," Mother said. "We promised not to betray Small's people. We cannot tell any of the warriors."

"We have to do something!"

"Yes. I'm thinking." She sat for a long time, staring at nothing. Small and I waited, watching her. Finally she stirred and looked at us each in turn. Then she smiled.

"We'll have a party."

Only my great faith in my mother prevented me from thinking she was crazy.

We began planning for a feast and made sure every family who had one of the Savages as a slave would be there. Mother visited them and encouraged them to bring all of their family members—but please, not their slaves, as we would be holding this party in our own courtyard, rather than a public building, and our complex was, after all, rather small. This feast was just for a few of our most important friends, she told them, so that we and Smoke Shell could thank them personally. With flattery and the subtle suggestion of gifts to be distributed to every guest, Mother soon got promises that all would attend. She even apologized to Three Deer and told her that we had a special gift for her, but it wouldn't be ready until the party.

Small went with her and gave whispered messages to the other Savages, telling them about the party since they could not understand much Mayan. To their leader he gave a map of the city that Mother and I drew on a bit of deerskin parchment. We had marked the best way out of the city, where they would pass few people. Small explained to them how they could get to the river, where they might find a boat docked just outside of town.

Small said he was trying to make up for leading the warriors to them. He did not tell our part in this, and although his people were suspicious, they could think of no reason he might be trying to trick them. They did not invite Small to join them, however.

We drew Feather Dawn and my father into the plot without their knowledge. Mother told Feather Dawn that this was a perfect chance to show off her wonderful weaving, as the very best families—most of them with eligible sons—would be at our feast. She enthusiastically began making belts and headdress bands to give out as gifts. Our father was less excited, but he agreed to supply some fine pottery. Mother and I meanwhile arranged the food, drink, and entertainment.

We had planned the feast with short notice, so the Savages wouldn't get impatient and try to escape sooner. By the day of the feast, I was a wreck, worried about what might go wrong and what we might have forgotten. At least I was too busy to worry about the feast itself. I hadn't even thought about what I was going to wear.

Our courtyard was full of activity, with hired cooks roasting a deer over an open fire and making piles of tortillas, and Feather Dawn supervising the decorations. Mother, Small, and I made an excuse that we needed something more from the market.

We did buy supplies, but instead of bringing them home, we slipped out of the city and to the river, where we had stashed an old canoe that my father no longer used. A few patches here and there had made it usable, and we stored food, fishhooks, and blankets inside. Mother didn't want the Savages attacking any farming villages because they were hungry.

Mother had asked Small how we could be sure the Savages wouldn't bring others back to attack the city in revenge. "No others," Small said. "Most men dead now. They only want home."

Finally, everything was ready but us. Mother and I

rushed to clean up, while Feather Dawn, resplendent in a new outfit she'd somehow had time to make herself, haughtily waited to greet the guests. I was looking critically at my best dress, a blue-and-white cotton one that everyone had already seen me in at every festival and that was getting noticeably too small, when Mother stuck her head around the sleeping partition.

"Almost forgot. Got you this," she said breathlessly, tossing a bunch of cloth at me before dashing off again.

I sorted it out and found a matching skirt, shawl, and headband in shades of blue and green, like the river and the sky. It wasn't as nice as the ones Feather Dawn made, but I was delighted anyway. They were the best clothes I had ever had, and I actually felt pretty.

The party itself is a blur in my memory. My face began to hurt from all the smiling, and much to my surprise, they weren't all fake smiles. I had a good time. The girls who had gone through their rite of passage to womanhood ignored me and hung around Feather Dawn, but several younger girls came. In the beginning I tried to keep myself busy helping serve the food and sometimes playing with the little children. Then Mother handed me a platter of sweets and told me to offer them to a group of girls my age. They smiled at me when I went over to them, and soon we were talking.

We admired the older boys and critiqued the older girls. "Your sister is really beautiful," Many Hands said, "but she seems vain."

"Still," Dark House said, "men don't care about that. She's gorgeous, and look at her weaving. I hope I get something she made."

They wanted to know all about Smoke Shell, too, and I proudly told them the story about how I had seen the Savages in the jungle.

"I'd heard that," said a tall, slender girl named Water Hummingbird, "but I thought it was just a rumor. Do you really get to go into the jungle alone? I'd never be allowed to."

"I wouldn't want to," Dark House said. "It's creepy in there. I like the city."

Many Hands, who was cute and plump, began talking about a visit she had made to Seven Caves, a huge city far to the south, but I wasn't really paying attention. Talking about the Savages had reminded me of why we were actually doing this. I looked around for Small, but couldn't see him in the crowd. I wondered if he had decided to try to join his friends after all. I hoped not. I liked him.

By the time the party ended, it was almost dawn. The last of our guests said good-bye, swaying from the effects of plenty of liquor and no sleep, and went home. We all fell into our beds. I was too tired to even think about the Savages.

I didn't wake up until midday. Mother and Small were in the courtyard, talking quietly. My father had already gone out somewhere, and Feather was still asleep. I groggily dragged myself out of bed, washed my face and hands, and changed clothes.

Mother handed me some tortillas when I joined them in the courtyard.

"What do you think happened?" I whispered.

"We haven't heard anything yet, and we can't go ask. We'll just have to wait."

The news came before I had finished eating. Smoke Shell ran through the door, calling for my parents. He spotted us in the courtyard and rushed out, stopping suddenly when he saw Small.

"You're still here!" he said with obvious surprise.

"Where else would he be?" Mother asked innocently.

"I thought . . ." Smoke Shell regained his composure. "All the other Savages have escaped. The news started coming just a little while ago. They must have sneaked out during the night, but no one noticed until after they got up this morning."

"Oh, dear!" Mother exclaimed. "Was anyone hurt?"

"One Mayan slave was killed. The old man who has been with Black Butterfly for years. He must have tried to stop them. Three other Mayan slaves are missing, but they must have gone with the Savages, or at least used the opportunity to escape. I can't blame them. They worked for Lord Holy Sweat Bath."

"What do you mean?" I asked.

"You know. He's not always nice to his slaves."

"I am sorry about the old slave," Mother said. "What are they planning to do?"

"They're sending a war party, only this time everyone wants to be part of it. Great Skull Zero wants us all in Longhouse so he can tell us what to do. Why the high priest is getting involved, I don't know. He's furious because most of the men who were here last night are half asleep and hung-over. They won't be ready for hours. The Savages will be long gone."

He turned suddenly to Small, who quickly replaced a smile with a blank expression.

"What do you know about all this?" Smoke Shell demanded.

"Now, darling," Mother said gently, "you know he doesn't speak much Mayan yet. He probably didn't understand anything you just said. In any case, he was here all last night."

"Yes, I suppose that's why he didn't get out, too. You'd better watch him."

"I don't think he would be very welcome back with his people."

Smoke Shell considered. "No, I guess not. Well, at least we got out of this easily. People will fuss for a while, but it's good gossip more than anything. Anyway, I have to go. I'm supposed to lead one of the search parties."

With a flash of smile and a wave, he trotted through the house, patting Feather Dawn on the head as she sat up to ask sleepily what was the matter.

Mother, Small, and I looked at one another. Smiles crept over our faces and became broad grins. We had succeeded with only one life lost. The Savages were free, the Mayan nobles were unhurt, and Lord Holy Sweat Bath had lost a few extra slaves, which served him right. And we had gotten a fun party out of it. I felt closer than ever to Mother, and to Small, too. I wondered if we would ever share this secret with anyone else. I hoped it would stay just ours.

ing Flint Sky God ordered a monument to the victory over the Savages, a tree-stone placed in the plaza. It was a column of stone as tall as two men and bigger across than the length of my arm.

When it was finished, Smoke Shell took me to see it and explained the carvings to me. His name was there, along one side, with a carved picture of him leading the warriors in battle. The other side had a battle scene, with Mayan warriors holding Savages by the hair and forcing them to kneel. Smoke Shell said that the battle wasn't quite like that, but the important thing was that the pictures represented the idea of the victory.

The front had a larger-than-life image of King Flint Sky God, and a passage about how the Savages were defeated during his reign. The back was covered with symbols telling the story of the battle. They didn't mention the Savages' escape. Smoke Shell said that wasn't important. We had won the war, and they wouldn't bother us anymore.

By then Smoke Shell was the most popular young man in the city. Young women were taught to lower their eyes, turn their backs, and step aside when a man passed, but they sighed and cast adoring glances after Smoke Shell—all the unmarried ones and some of the married ones, too.

Smoke Shell was too busy to take a wife. He learned everything that he could. When he came to visit, he taught me how to count and a little about the calendar and the stars. When we walked past the stone pillars that commemorated important events, Smoke Shell explained what the symbols meant and how to read the dates.

"See these bars? A bar stands for five, the number of fingers you have on one hand. The dots are one each. So this bar with two dots means seven. Your age would be two bars and one dot."

Counting was easy, but the calendar was nearly impossible to understand. The Calendar Round is made of two interlocked calendars: the Count of Days and the Civil Year. The Count of Days is the 260-day sacred year that determines ceremonial life. Each day is assigned a number from one to thirteen, plus one of twenty day names. The day names tell you what god is associated with each day, and what you can expect from the day. I learned to recite the days and the clues to their meanings, starting from any-where in the list, as there is no beginning or end to the circle, just whatever number happens to fall on that day.

For example, one month you might count out:

One Deer—the motherfathers
Two Yellow—ripening, spoiling
Three Thunder—paying, suffering
Four Dog—jealousy, uncertainty
Five Monkey—spinning thread
Six Tooth—the good road, the bad road
Seven Cane—in the house
Eight Jaguar—before the Holy World
Nine Bird—praying, pleading, gold and silver
Ten Sinner—before God
Eleven Thought—good thoughts, bad thoughts
Twelve Blade—lies and concealment
Thirteen Rain—filling the bowl, setting the table

Then the numbers start over, but the names continue.

One Marksman—honor the dead
Two Left-handed—going mad
Three Wind—getting angry
Four Foredawn—opening, blaming
Five Net—a burden, a debt
Six Snake—day of the enemy
Seven Death—unexpected favors

And then the day names start over, and the numbers keep going: Eight Deer, Nine Yellow, Ten Thunder. The priests who study the calendar can count backward as well as forward, far into the past or future, and they can tell you all the subtle meanings in the days. The number associated with the day intensifies its power, so that One Net may bring a small debt, while Thirteen Net brings a huge one.

The thirteen numbers and twenty day names rotate, interlocking for 260 total combinations; the Count of Days lasts the same amount of time it takes for a baby to be born after its mother first knows the child is inside her. The Civil Year, for ordinary affairs, has 365 days divided into 18 months of 20 days, plus an extra 5 days. The Civil Year contains one complete change of seasons.

When the two calendars combine to form the Calendar Round, you have a fifty-two-year cycle before you come back to the exact same day name and date. Then there's the Long Count, which tracks time through our entire history. When Smoke Shell mentioned that one, I just gave up.

Smoke Shell was smart enough to understand most of the complicated calendrics, mathematics, and astronomy, and his popularity kept rising. He didn't take all the credit for the victory, though. The other warriors from his house rose in status and popularity with him, though not as far, and they were wildly loyal to Smoke Shell.

My parents could have stopped working at trade and lived like other nobles, my father acting as a courtier for the king and getting our supplies from the store-houses full of the goods people paid as taxes. Feather Dawn thought they should, that trade was now beneath us.

But Mother could never give up her medicine, especially when people still needed her. I was glad because I enjoyed working with her and learning. I would have been bored otherwise. Mother became a popular healer for the nobility. She grumbled behind their backs and said all they really wanted was to be able to say they knew Smoke Shell's family and per-haps to arrange a marriage with one of their daugh-ters, but they gave her nice gifts, which enabled her to treat the poor peasants for free.

My father retired for about two months. He didn't like government work, though. He would go to meet-ings for a little while, then get bored and head over to the market. He spent most of his time there.

Sometimes Mother sent me to the market to look for my father, and I could understand why he enjoyed it so much. You could find anything in the market, gold jewelry, precious stones, jaguar skins, tunics covered with colorful feathers or animal fur, and decorated shields, as well as the goods needed for everyday life.

I always stopped to look at the medicine stalls, with their pots and baskets full of roots, seeds, maguey leaves, tobacco, and copal resin. The skins and flesh of snakes were spread on reed mats in bunches. You could find medicines to treat everything from stiff joints to gout.

I liked the beautiful caged tropical birds, too, noisy toucans with dark red, black, and yellow feathers and enormous beaks, or sociable parrots with bright blue, green, red, and yellow feathers. The only bird you didn't see was the quetzal because it would die if kept in a cage. That's why the quetzal represents the Mayan people, with our pride and fierce spirit.

People bartered what they had for what they need-ed, or they used copper axes, cocoa beans, red beans, stone or shell beads, or feathers for money. Supervisors regulated prices, while judges arbitrated disputes or dealt with theft.

The pottery stalls were placed together, with stacks of bowls, goblets, and pots, some plain and others ornately decorated. That's where I'd find my father, visiting with old friends and debating the quality of the various ceramics.

Finally, my father got so restless he started working

again. He was used to traveling a lot, and he enjoyed the freedom. I guess once you're used to working, it's not so easy to stop. At least if you enjoy what you do.

My father's trading business improved because it was now safer to go on trading missions to the coast and the mountains and because people were willing to spend money more freely, believing that soon we would all be prosperous again. Plus, other nobles tended to choose Father's pottery over that of ordinary merchants because they felt it gave them more status to buy from a noble.

So my father returned to his trade routes. Sometimes he followed the White Roads, broad raised cement paths that led from our city to the outlying districts, taking slaves and helpers to carry the goods. A few times a year he made major trips to far-off kingdoms.

The peasants who had flooded the city returned to their villages. Since there were no longer so many injured peasants to treat, Mother joined Father on some of his big trips, and she took me along.

We traveled in a group with five or six other merchants who traded flint, honey, cotton textiles, tobacco, or rubber, exchanging them for obsidian blades, jewelry, jade, and metalwork from the highlands, or salt, shells, dried fish, stingray spines, and pearls from the coast. We went down the river in long, thin dugout canoes each carved from a single piece of some hardwood like mahogany, with our merchandise piled inside. Each man brought along a slave or two to help carry the goods.

Small went with us. He was an expert with the canoe because his people lived on islands far out in the ocean and used canoes for travel. He worked hard, and he was kind to me. Small thought Mother was practically a goddess, and he would do anything she asked, partly out of fear and partly out of respect. He learned Mayan well, although he kept a thick accent.

He seemed happy enough, but he didn't like to talk of the home he would never see again. He said only that his people were pretty much like us, living in thatched huts, farming, playing ball, and holding religious ceremonies. Their villages were smaller than our cities, though, and they didn't have human sacrifices. They were usually peaceful, he said, but his island had lost all its crops in a terrible storm, so bands of young men were sent to look for food or for riches that could be traded for food. They had been harsh because they were scared, he said, and because the meanest men somehow always became the leaders.

Once I asked Small if he missed his family. He was quiet for a while. "I'm an orphan," he finally said. "I did what other people said in order to get scraps of food. Finally I was old enough to get my own food, and there was no food left. So now . . . No, I have no

family to miss." He was silent then, staring over the water, and I didn't ask more.

During our journeys, Mother and I looked for medicinal plants along the river, traded for more at our destination, and talked with people to see if we could learn any new treatments. I loved traveling, meeting people, and seeing new cities.

Gliding almost silently down the river, we sometimes saw animals along the shore. Birds often rose up at our approach, from large vultures and mottled owls to tiny hummingbirds and wrens, and, of course, the bright toucans, parrots, and quetzals. Groups of up to twenty spider monkeys, with light patches around their eyes and mouths and round black faces, would run along the branches or swing by their long thin arms and tails. Howler monkeys, disturbed by our approach, would roar deafeningly from the trees. They were about the size of four-year-old children, with reddish fur and powerful tails as long as their bodies.

We had to watch for crocodiles lurking in the muddy water, looking like half-submerged logs until they moved. The larger ones could easily overturn a canoe and drag away its occupant before he had time to draw a club.

Once in a while we saw an armadillo, anteater, or herd of peccaries that had come to take a drink, or even a jaguar, its lean, graceful body covered in golden brown fur speckled with black. When traveling through the jungle on foot, I had to make noise to warn the animals of my approach so I wouldn't meet such a creature, but from the safety of the canoe I loved seeing them.

Sometimes we brought the canoes close to shore and plucked bright green iguanas from the drooping tree branches that hung over the water. I'd hold the funny lizards, with long toes, spines down the back, and flaps of skin hanging under their throats, until we made camp and cooked them for dinner.

I even saw the ocean. It was so beautiful I could hardly believe it, every shade of blue and green, from pale and milky to deep and brilliant. I thought I had risen to the upperworld. I splashed in the water at the edge and learned to swim a little, something few at home could do. I watched the fishermen drag nets through the water or cast lines with hooks of cactus thorn, bone, or shell. I dug in the sand for clams, and we had fish from the sea for the first time. Before we'd only had fish from the river, and not often that.

Feather Dawn stayed home, of course. We usually passed the night at farming villages along the river, the local patriarch or priest generously welcoming us into his house, but even this was too uncivilized for my sister. She began wearing all the jewelry she could get her hands on and wearing her hair in a different elaborate style each day. The parents of young noblemen sent matchmakers to arrange a marriage, but Feather Dawn was holding out for someone really important. Mother was in no rush to marry her off, and my father didn't pay much attention to those things, so they let Feather have her way.

I thought all the glittering baubles actually hid her real beauty and made her look more like any of the other noble girls, but I didn't tell her. She wove gorgeous cloth from delicate yarn and embroidered it extravagantly. Most of it she sold or traded for jewelry. The best she kept for herself or Smoke Shell.

She never made anything for me. She said I was too young to need nice things, even though I was only a year younger than she was and she had wanted and worn nice things for years. She said I would just get them dirty anyway, which was true, but I would have liked to have some fancy clothes for festivals. I would never ask Feather Dawn for anything, though, and she wouldn't believe Smoke Shell when he said I was partly responsible for her new status. Some things don't change.

ing Flint Sky God got sick the year I turned twelve. We were sorry that he was sick, but a little excited, too, because of what it might mean for Smoke Shell. King Flint Sky God had no living sons or brothers to inherit his throne. People said that Smoke Shell might become the next king when King Flint Sky God died. I tried not to think about that because it made me feel guilty. I had plenty to keep my mind busy, anyway, with my Descent of the Gods ceremony approaching.

When a girl reaches age five, her mother ties a string with a red shell dangling from it around her daughter's waist. Boys get a white bead braided into their hair at the same age. These are symbols of virginity and must not be removed until the Descent of the Gods, a rite of passage into adulthood.

The high priest picked a lucky day for the ceremony—the day Twelve Tooth, the same day the Lords of Death were sacrificed to the Hero Twins. All the twelve-year-old girls and fourteen-year-old boys participated. A lord named Curl Snout sponsored the children that year, helping the priest during the ceremony and holding the feast. An old man was chosen to be the boys' godfather, and an old woman was godmother to me and the other girls.

Curl Snout's house was cleaned, then the priest drove out any evil spirits, and the house was cleaned again. The ceremony was held in the courtyard, which was spread with fresh leaves. Over one hundred children took part, so it was crowded. When I entered, I passed Great Skull Zero. He studied me for a moment in puzzlement, then he nodded in recognition.

"Hello, child," he said. "You are indeed growing up. Do you see your brother often?"

"Yes," I answered. "No—I mean, not as often as I'd like." I was flustered that such an important man would notice me.

"He is very busy these days." The high priest smiled and moved on, and Mother took my arm to direct me to my place in the courtyard.

Everyone was excited, children and parents both. Finally we all settled down enough for the ceremony to begin. Four rain chiefs, lesser priests, placed squares of white cloth on each of our heads. Great Skull Zero asked us each if we had committed any sins. No one said they had. We would have had to leave if we did. I thought wildly of all the little things I had done, but I was pretty sure they weren't serious enough.

Great Skull Zero gave us a blessing and used a carved stick with rattlesnake tails hanging from it to sprinkle water on us. I still had the cloth over my head, but I could see through it a little. Curl Snout went around to each child with a bone Great Skull Zero gave him. When he reached me, he tapped my forehead nine times with the bone, then spread a wet mixture of ground cocoa and pollen on my forehead and between my fingers and toes. It tickled a little between the toes, but I forced myself not to laugh.

Finally Great Skull Zero took the cloth off our heads. We gave the rain chiefs gifts of cocoa beans and feathers, then the high priest snipped the beads from the boys' hair. The rain chiefs smoked pipes and they gave us each a puff or two. I coughed when I tried the pipe, and some boys laughed at me, but one of them coughed, too. Our mothers passed out gifts of food, and a special official drank a cup of alcoholic balché in one long draught as an offering to the gods.

Then my mother joined me and cut off my red shell, as the other mothers were doing for their daughters. I felt the absence of that string and shell for days, as if I had forgotten to put on my skirt, but the sensation was a thrilling reminder. I had become a woman.

Our parents stayed to feast and drink balché, giving gifts of cotton cloth to the priests and officials. You would think that we would be permitted to join

them, since we had just officially become adults, but we were sent home.

I got some nice gifts, though. Smoke Shell gave me some jade earplugs, pale blue and white like a cloudy sky, with a matching necklace of small beads. Feather Dawn gave me a water gourd painted with a black-and-orange design, and from my father I got an incense burner, the clay delicately etched and painted with a scene of a woman painting another woman's face, her long arm reaching out with the slender paintbrush.

Small didn't have any money, of course, but he carved me a figure out of wood, just big enough to fit in my hand. He said it was one of the gods of his people and would bring me luck.

I got a special meal at home, too: turkey rubbed with chili and roasted over the fire; a stew of pumpkin, red beans, tomatoes, and avocado; rabbit-meat tamales; bananas; papayas; and cocoa sweetened with honey and vanilla.

We finally had plenty of food again that year, meat and exotic trade items, too, although the storehouses weren't yet full. People had grown tired of scrimping during the war, so when we finally had enough, we used it. As soon as the peasants started to fill the storehouses with their taxes of grain, fruit, or meat, the nobles would empty them again, throwing great feasts and public celebrations. Great Skull Zero sponsored a lot of those, gaining prestige for himself. The king was usually too sick to participate.

Nothing much really changed after the Descent of the Gods, although the ceremony meant that we were old enough to marry. Parents would hire match-makers to arrange marriages for their children, but most girls didn't get married for two or three more years. Boys would marry at about eighteen.

After the Descent of the Gods, the boys moved out of their parents' homes to live in one of the young men's communal houses, and they began painting themselves black to signify that they were bachelors. Girls still lived at home and were supposed to continue learning cooking, spinning, weaving, and keeping house.

I wasn't anxious to get married, because then I would have to stay home and cook and clean. I was happier foraging in the jungle for medicine, learning healing from my mother, and sometimes traveling with my father. Still, my mother decided it was time I learned how to keep house.

I never could weave on a loom, but I could make a decent grass mat for the floor. I found I actually enjoyed cooking, probably because I enjoyed eating. Even grinding corn didn't bother me. It was repetitive, but that meant my mind could wander freely. I learned to make stews, flavoring them with dried chilies I crushed in a little stone mortar, and tamales, stuffing corn dough with meat or vegetables, wrapping the pieces in cornhusks, and steaming them.

Mother decided I would be all right as long as I could cook and clean and knew medicine well enough to work as a healer. That way I could work in trade for the textiles I needed for my family and to pay taxes.

Smoke Shell finally did get married, a few months after I turned thirteen, to a woman named Double Bird. Even I, who thought my brother deserved the very best in everything, most of all in a wife, could find no fault with her. She was pretty, with lively black eyes, delicate high cheekbones, creamy brown skin, and glossy black hair that reached almost to her knees when she let it loose. She was small, not much bigger than I was, although she was several years older. She had a musical voice, and she liked me.

Her family was not one of the richest, but her father was a lord and a nephew of the king, so the match was politically a good one. That's not why Smoke Shell finally decided to marry, however. He knew Double Bird a little from visits to her father, so he knew she was nice, and smart, and wasn't too shy to talk to him. Most men wouldn't have cared, since husbands and wives usually spend very little time together and don't even talk much. Smoke Shell was different, though. He had taught me writing and counting, and I knew he would want a wife at least as educated as his little sister.

Many girls wept on Smoke Shell's wedding day, but our family was full of joy. King Flint Sky God was weak from his long illness, but Great Skull Zero delivered some lovely presents from the king, including two matching cylindrical vases with painted scenes of dancers.

Normally a man has to work for his father-in-law for several years before he is allowed to establish his own home, but because Smoke Shell was so busy with government work, he just paid a good bride price. Double Bird's family probably would have given her away for nothing so long as she married Smoke Shell, but my brother was always generous.

All their friends and relatives helped to build a home for Smoke Shell and Double Bird and to stock it with everything they would need. We worked for two days, stopping only to eat, drink, and sleep, and gave them a nice large house with two rooms. We used limestone plaster to seal the floors and roof, then mixed in some paint and covered the outer walls in a dazzling coat of yellow plaster. We filled their home with pottery, water gourds, baskets and bags, wooden chests, tools, and a grinding stone.

Then the wedding ceremony began. This was an important marriage, so Great Skull Zero was the priest. He greeted our family warmly, then led Smoke Shell and Double Bird into their new home. The high priest lit a ball of incense and made a fire in the hearth. The scented smoke drifted around Smoke Shell and Double Bird as they sat on a mat facing each other. Great Skull Zero recited a short sermon honoring the marriage and praying for healthy children. Then he waved us all away from the house and we left the newlyweds alone. They had to sit in silence, looking into the fire until it went out. The rest of us were busy celebrating at our house and didn't see them again until the next day.

They joined Double Bird's family complex, which was a large one gathered around a central courtyard. She had three sisters and five brothers, most younger, but one brother was a friend of Smoke Shell. Two of Double Bird's grandparents were still alive. They must have been over fifty, maybe even close to sixty. Only the well-off Maya have a chance of living that long, and not too many of them make it, so the family must have been rich and lucky. The grandparents had their own house in the complex, although the children did most of the work for them.

Double Bird's aunts had brought their husbands to live there years before, and they had many children between them. Their complex was always busy and full of noise. I enjoyed visiting and playing with my young in-laws.

Smoke Shell and Double Bird were happy together, and a few months later Double Bird was pregnant.

Not long after we found out about the coming baby, I returned from a trip to the jungle to find a visitor in my house. I was embarrassed to go in, because my hair was tangled and I had scratches on my arms and legs from gathering papaya. The papaya tree has a tall, slender bare trunk; all the branches and fruit are high at the top. I could see this one huge, luscious-looking fruit that would not be shaken down, so I climbed a neighboring tree. I held on to the vines that twisted around it, and then reached out for the fruit with one hand while holding on behind me with the other and gripping with both legs.

I got that papaya, the most perfect one I had ever seen, and several others, plus some breadfruit, bananas, and medicinal roots from my foraging. A very productive day, but not one that left me clean or pretty.

I slipped into the house quietly, put down my basket, and edged along the wall until I reached the door to the courtyard, where my family and the visitor were. I peeked out and saw Feather Dawn sitting with her head down, looking demure, but flushed and smiling. Mother and Father looked pleased as well. They were thanking the visitor, who was preparing to leave. When she turned, I recognized her as a professional matchmaker.

They came to the doorway, and I darted back behind the partition to our sleeping area. Everyone thanked everyone else profusely, and the matchmaker left. They watched her walk away, and then Feather Dawn jumped up and down with a shriek of excitement.

I stepped out to join them. Feather stopped and looked at me critically.

"Eveningstar, I do hope you'll be able to come to my wedding with clean arms."

"Congratulations," I said. "And who is the lucky one?"

"Six Sky Monkey." She sank to the floor with a contented sigh.

She had reason to rejoice. Six Sky Monkey was one of the warriors who had gone after the Savages with Smoke Shell. He had risen in prestige since then and recently had been named a lord. Plus, he was handsome.

"That's nice," I said.

I picked up my basket and went into the courtyard to sort and clean my finds. Mother followed me a minute later.

"Your sister has made a very good match."

"I know."

"You mustn't be jealous. Your time will come."

"I'm happy for her."

I concentrated on my basket so I could hide the hot moisture in my eyes. Mother was silent for a minute.

"You found some nice things today. That large papaya looks delicious."

I determined to press down the jealousy and hurt rising inside me. After a struggle, I said, "Feather Dawn can have it with dinner. To celebrate."

"My darling little duck. I know you will always be all right. Feather is not so strong. She needs more."

"She'll always get it," I said, stroking the smooth, orange skin of the perfect papaya I held in my hands. "But she won't appreciate it."

"True. But there are more reasons for giving than to be thanked."

he first day of that year had been Thirteen Wind, and so the year was called Thirteen Wind also. Lord Wind is known to get angry and even go mad. Sometimes he possesses people during his years, especially when the number is high, and thirteen is the highest. We should have expected great madness that year, especially with a king dying. But we were wrapped up in our own affairs, and life seemed full of possibilities.

While we were preparing for Feather's wedding, King Flint Sky God died. Smoke Shell came to tell us, bursting in as we were stretching and dressing and Mother was warming the tortillas for breakfast.

My brother's eyes shone as he gave us the somber news, and I shivered with excitement. Feather Dawn was not even trying to hide her smile, and a rich tremor in Mother's voice betrayed the sad words she spoke.

"He will be missed."

We nodded in agreement, but still our eyes shone. I remembered the faceless old king, with his thin ankles under the glorious costume. We were all sorry King Flint Sky God had died; he'd been a good king and our family had prospered under him. Smoke Shell had known him well and loved him.

Yet we could not deny the current of excitement underneath our sorrow. The king had no heirs, so the nobles would chose one from among themselves. Smoke Shell was a likely candidate. His father-in-law was another possibility, and Feather Dawn must have imagined that her young fiancé was as well.

Great Skull Zero had declared a period of mourning. We would find out after that.

That night I dreamed of the old king. My family gathered around him as he lay on a great stone altar. He was wearing his green quetzal feather tunic and headdress and all his jewelry, and an embroidered cloth lay over his face. I thought he was dead, but then he sat up. He got off the altar, and Smoke Shell went forward to help him. The king leaned on Smoke Shell's arm and led him away. They started walking up some stone steps. The steps kept going, high into the sky, farther than I could see. They walked together up the steps until they were out of sight.

The next morning I told my mother and Feather Dawn about the dream.

Feather was excited. "It means that Smoke Shell will rise up to become a king, like King Flint Sky God," she said.

Mother looked troubled, but she only said, "We shall see."

I remembered that the new day was Two Net, a day for paying debts. But we had no debts to pay.

The summons came soon after. Great Skull Zero wanted all the noble families to gather in the central plaza. We put on our best clothes and jewelry and hurried there alongside other noble families. As an important family, we were let through the crowd to the front, where we stood near Smoke Shell and Double Bird.

When we had all assembled, Great Skull Zero came out of the Temple of Ah Puch, the Lord of Death. The priest stood at the top of the temple steps, looking down on us, with the colorful stone carvings of the Lord of Death on either side of him. The autumn drizzle had let up, and sunlight glared off his gold breastplate and headdress so that we could barely see his face. His voice boomed out over the crowd.

"I, Great Skull Zero, the high priest, have spoken to the gods. I have prayed to Itzamna, Chac, and Ah Puch. They have given me a mission. Will you help me to complete it?"

We murmured our agreement. Of course we would do as the gods and their messenger required.

"I have asked them about the burial of King Flint Sky God. He was our father, our leader, our god. He ruled us wisely for many years. He must have a special burial."

We all agreed. We would do anything necessary to help the king in his journey to the upperworld, where he would join the other gods.

"King Flint Sky God must be buried with young men to serve him."

For most ceremonies, sacrificial victims were slaves, enemy soldiers, criminals, or orphans purchased from the villages. For the king, his servants might be buried with him, or perhaps some of the less important children of noble families. I hoped that Small would not be chosen, although he would make a good symbol of the War with the Savages.

"These must not be just any men. King Flint Sky God deserves our very best to serve him."

In the crowd, people began glancing at each other nervously. I remembered my dream and felt sick.

"The gods have given me the names of the six who must accompany the king. You will come forward now.

"Stormy Sky."

A murmur rose up from one section of the crowd.

"Jaguar Paw Skull."

Another group began to wail. I knew the man. He was a friend of my brother.

"Red Macaw."

Exclamations of surprise were sweeping the crowd. Red Macaw was an important leader and confidant of the king.

"Snake Bird."

Another of the city's top men, a lord who had served since before I was born.

"Six Sky Monkey."

Feather Dawn shrieked and sank to the ground as her fiancé's name was called. She kept screaming, pausing only long enough to gather breath for the next wail. I strained to hear the last name called.

"Smoke Shell."

The temple in front of me began to blur and I swayed, barely staying on my feet. I heard the cries of the crowd as if through a fog. I gave up and sank to the ground. I felt as if the gods were pressing on my chest from all sides, trying to squeeze the breath from me.

When my vision cleared, I searched for Smoke Shell. He was standing straight, his face solemn and pale, supporting the pregnant Double Bird, who had fainted in his arms.

"You will come forward now," Great Skull Zero shouted.

Smoke Shell gently set Double Bird on the ground. She began to awaken, and he kissed her. I scrambled to my feet and rushed to them. I knelt next to Double Bird, tears running down my face. Smoke Shell looked at me.

"Take care of her," he said.

He turned and began walking up the steps. I

supported Double Bird with my arm as we watched him go.

The other men slowly joined him. When they reached Great Skull Zero, they turned and looked down at their wives, parents, children, brothers, sisters, and friends, weeping in the plaza below.

Great Skull Zero's voice roared.

"Silence! The gods have demanded these men in sacrifice. They have received the greatest honor, to die with their king. You must let them go willingly or risk angering the gods. We have suffered greatly in recent years—war, famine, sickness. The gods have finally forgiven us. Do you want to go back to that? We will begin the fasting and purification immediately. The burial will be in ten days, on the day Twelve Jaguar."

He turned and stepped back into the darkness of the temple. After a moment, the men followed him. We stayed in the plaza for some time, too shocked to move. Some wept softly, while others stared with empty gazes at the temple stairs. Finally, those who were not related to any of the sacrificial victims began to leave, moving quietly and not looking at the tortured faces around them.

When only close family members and tree-stones were left in the plaza, the rest of us began to stir. I helped Double Bird to her feet. Mother joined us. She had been comforting Feather Dawn, but now she turned her attention to Double Bird, afraid the shock would harm the baby. We each took an arm, leaving my father to drag Feather home. Double Bird turned her wet face toward Mother.

"How can I live?"

"You must be brave, as Smoke Shell was."

 e took Double Bird home to live with us, so Mother could watch over her and the baby. Mother thought the best cure for grief was activity, so she pushed us all to keep busy. The only way she could get Feather Dawn to stop lying around crying was to give her an almost impossible task: weave new cloaks for Smoke Shell and Six Sky Monkey in time for the burial.

Feather Dawn threw herself into the work, sitting at her loom from dawn until late at night, stopping only to drink a little cornmeal and water or eat a few bites of tortilla. Sometimes her fingers started shaking and she would bury her face in her hands and cry in great sobs. But when her breath came more easily again, she would resume work, determined that Smoke Shell and Six Sky Monkey would go into the next world with the most magnificent cloaks ever made and those from her own small hands.

Double Bird did whatever she was told, whether it was grinding corn or sweeping the courtyard, but someone had to watch her to make sure she would stop as well. She worked with no expression on her face, staring far beyond the tools in front of her. She would keep grinding one handful of corn until it was fine as dust, or sweep one spot in the courtyard until she began to wear a hole in the stone.

Mother found jobs for me, too, sending me after hard-to-find medicines that she suddenly needed, even though the only illness she was treating was our own family's grief. No one else dared come to her, for they would have had to say something about Smoke Shell, and what was there to say? But I went after the medicine anyway, sometimes finding it and sometimes just wandering in the jungle in the rain.

Mother sent Small with me, supposedly to help me but really to watch over me. He didn't try to talk much, just kept me from stepping on a snake or stumbling over a jaguar while I mourned in silence.

Mother prayed. She went to the Temple of Ix Chel whenever she thought she could leave Double Bird and Feather Dawn alone, and when she could not, she prayed at home, at our courtyard shrine or as she went about her work.

I could not speak to the gods. I felt betrayed, and it was all I could do not to hate them.

On the day before King Flint Sky God's burial, I was walking aimlessly along the swollen, gurgling river. Howler monkeys let out grunting roars above, but their long furry limbs were hidden by the towering layers of branches overhead. I pushed aside a dangling vine and came out into a clearing. Human bones, picked clean and broken by jaguars, foxes, and wild dogs, lay in jumbled piles, glistening in the drizzle. I stared at them in wonder and then noticed Small staring, too, his face tight with grief.

"These were your friends," I said with sudden realization.

He nodded sadly. "Never buried. I should have come to bury them. My fault."

"We'll bury them now," I said softly.

We had no tools but my digging stick. We took turns, one of us tearing away vines and moving stones while the other brushed aside the spongy fungi and dug into the rich wet earth, full of burrowing insects. The bones were scattered and mingled, so we buried them all together.

Small used his simple cloak as a shroud, spreading it in the hole. We gathered the slender sticks that had once supported living bodies, brushed off the moss and dirt, and laid them together. Then we folded the cloak over them, pushed the dirt over the top with our hands, and patted down the mound.

We stood for several minutes staring at the small lump as water ran off our hair and faces. It didn't seem like much for half a day's work. It seemed even less for nineteen lives. I said a silent prayer for them and went to the river to wash up so Small could be alone with his thoughts.

He joined me a while later and scrubbed the mud off his arms and legs while I sat staring at the water and the dense canopy of green on the other side, listening to the chirps and warbles of the birds. A quetzal separated from the trees and flew along the river, its shimmering tail feathers forming a graceful arc three times as long as its body. Around its crimson chest, the green feathers of its wings and back looked almost blue in the muted light. Somewhere a puma cried out, a low rough call like a woman moaning.

"I don't understand any of this," I said. "What does it all mean?"

Small looked at me solemnly. "I do not know these things. Ask the gods. Only the gods know."

We walked back in silence, he thinking of a past tragedy and I of a future one. We left the jungle and passed by farmers tending their fields just as if it were an ordinary day. Through the gray mist over the city, I saw the Temple of Ix Chel, seeming small and plain against the grander temples behind it.

Small waited for me outside while I walked the short flight of steps and entered the cool, dim prayer room. Above the altar an image of the aged, toothless goddess sat in a moon sign with her bone jewelry, headdress of tangled snakes, and jaguar claws for toenails. I took out the few fruits and herbs I had gathered that morning and laid them down as an offering. Then I took off one of the necklaces I wore and laid the string of onyx and silver beads on the altar, kneeling before it in a puddle from my wet clothes.

I could not think of the proper prayers. My heart and mind were filled with only one thought.

Why?

I sank into a meditation so deep I lost all track of time and all track of myself. When I finally came back to this world, I could barely see the altar. The doorway behind me was only a lighter shadow in the blackness. Ix Chel had answered my question, but I didn't understand the answer. To the gods, there was no reason.

I rose slowly on cramped legs and descended the staircase feeling exhausted and weak. Small sat at the bottom, glistening with dampness, his bare arms wrapped around his legs, shivering in the cool night air. He rose when he saw me.

"The gods don't have a reason, either," I said.

Small nodded, as if he had expected this answer.

"Then you ask Mother."

Feather Dawn was still sitting at her loom, weaving by the light of a torch. She didn't see us as we passed her. Double Bird and my father were in their beds. I heard a low voice coming from the courtyard and went through to find Mother kneeling there, mumbling soft prayers. Small sank into a crouch against the wall and sat in silence. I knelt next to Mother.

For a long time we stared into the darkness. The rain let up, but the air itself still felt moist. Suddenly I could control myself no longer.

"Mother, do you really believe the gods demanded Smoke Shell in sacrifice?"

She looked at me without answering. When she finally spoke, her voice was low.

"No. I have prayed for many hours, and my heart tells me that this is wrong."

"Then what is Great Skull Zero doing? We must tell him he has made a mistake."

"It is not a mistake to Great Skull Zero. He knows that the people would have made Smoke Shell king. Once he has removed Smoke Shell, along with his strongest supporters, Great Skull Zero will be the most powerful man in the city."

"But why? What does he want?"

"Great Skull Zero is too proud to answer to a young king. For years, he made many decisions for King Flint Sky God. He doesn't want to lose that power."

"What can we do?"

Her shoulders slumped and her face sank. For the first time, I thought my mother looked old, and beaten.

"We can do nothing. We might get the families of

some of the victims to join us, but most people will be too afraid of the gods to challenge Great Skull Zero. If we had more time . . . but there is no time. Great Skull Zero has made sure of that."

"That's why the burial is so soon."

"Yes. So we have no time to mount a challenge, and Smoke Shell and the other men have no time to realize what Great Skull Zero is doing."

"If we could tell them . . ."

"Even then, I don't know. It is very hard to challenge a high priest. Only the king can do that, and there is no king."

I had not cried freely since I heard Great Skull Zero call Smoke Shell's name. At last the pain welled up inside me to overflowing. I laid my head in Mother's lap, and she wrapped her arms around me, softly stroking my hair as my body shook with sobs.

 had last seen Smoke Shell at the Temple of Ah Puch, so that was where I would go to find him. I lay in the dark, staring at nothing and making plans, listening to the familiar sounds of breathing from my family, my mother's heavy sighs, my father's occasional snoring, and my sister's light nasal whine. From beyond the walls came the sounds of night in the city: dogs snuffling greetings to each other, ducks disturbed by the dogs resettling themselves in the courtyards, and now and then the slap of sandals on hard earth as a man passed in the street.

When the breathing around me had settled in steady rhythms and no human sounds filtered through the walls, I rose. I dressed in a dark brown skirt and shawl and tied my hair back with a black band. On bare feet I padded softly across the floor and slid the slender obsidian knife from Mother's medicine basket, tucking it into my waistband. I studied Mother's sleeping face for a moment, resisted the urge to touch her, and slipped out the door.

I had never been out on the streets that late. My eyes had adjusted to the darkness inside, and the night was bright by comparison, with a nearly full moon and just a few clouds. The Temple of Ah Puch rose above the houses on the edge of the plaza. It seemed farther away than it had been.

I stayed toward the edges of the street, feeling safer against the buildings. When I heard some scuffling, I flattened myself against a wall, hoping to blend in with the shadows. A dog rounded the corner, sniffed at my ankles, and went on.

As soon as I had relaxed, I caught something out of the corner of my eye and froze again. A shadow behind me had moved. The dog wandered over to the dark space between two buildings to investigate. He snuffed about, then continued his rounds. It had been nothing, or perhaps a spirit of the night.

By the time I got to the plaza, I could feel my heart pounding in my chest. I had seen no living thing, but a dozen demons seemed to threaten me. I stared at the looming dark shapes of tree-stones scattered about the plaza, convinced that one of them might really be a person or at least be hiding a person behind it.

Finally I forced myself to take slow, deep breaths, knowing that the danger would soon be much greater, and I had only my courage to carry me up the long flight of silvery gray steps and into the black hole at the top of the Temple of Ah Puch, Lord of Death.

I took a step forward.

Someone grabbed my arm.

I spun around, shoving a hand into my mouth to block a scream. The dark figure before me started, throwing his arms up in defense and stumbling backward. He tripped over his own feet and fell. Small sat there, looking dazed.

I giggled a little, in relief more than amusement, then knelt beside him.

"You frightened me," I whispered.

"Frightened me, too!"

"What are you doing?"

"Helping you."

"I'm going to warn Smoke Shell."

"I thought so. I stayed awake for you."

I studied him for a moment, this strange young man who was offering to risk his life to save the man who had killed his companions and forced his exile and slavery. I didn't understand Savages.

"Let's go, then. Quietly."

The temple stairs seemed endless, exposed as we were in the moonlight. I was torn between wanting to run, to reach the top faster and be out of sight, and wanting to move silently. Worried that guards might be lurking just inside the doorway, I chose stealth over speed, hoping to surprise them napping.

At the top, the black square of doorway loomed before us, looking darker than anything I'd ever seen.

What if there were guards, and they had seen us coming and were waiting there, just inside, ready to attack the moment we passed the sacred portal?

Small laid a hand gently on my arm, then stepped forward into the darkness. I could barely see his narrow figure in the gloom. He peered to each side. Nothing else moved.

I joined him, and we waited for our eyes to make what adjustment they could. I had never been in this temple and did not know the layout, so I began feeling along the walls. In the left back corner was a doorway. The corridor led right and then left.

I realized that across from the main entrance was a stone wall, but we had come around it and were now in a short passage leading directly away from the temple steps. A faint light glowed at the end. I gripped Small's arm with cold fingers as we walked, our bare feet silent on the smooth stone but our breathing sounding like a hurricane to my oversensitive ears.

The corridor opened into a room with an altar directly across from us. Dim torches flickered on either side. We peeked around the corners and found the room empty. Although no doorways were visible, I felt certain there must be some.

Bright tapestries hung on either side of the doorway we had just come through. They depicted the Lord of Death, with his skeletal nose and jaw, his spine bare of flesh, and his decaying, speckled body, intricately woven in rich reds, white, and black. Before him dying men knelt in agony, while the creatures of the underworld grinned below.

I carefully pulled back the tapestry to the left and saw nothing but stone. I tried the one on the right, revealing a passage behind it. The light from the torches penetrated only a few feet. I considered taking a torch with me, but I did not want to risk offending Ah Puch, and besides, light could give us away.

Small and I clung to each other, feeling the walls with our free arms. We were so busy with our hands that our feet nearly betrayed us.

I put a foot forward and stepped into space.

My gasp warned Small, and he jerked me back before I could fall. Feeling more carefully, we discovered that we had come to a flight of stairs.

With our bare feet to guide us, we descended into the depths of the Temple of the Lord of Death. At the bottom, I put out a hand and felt walls ahead of us and to our right. To our left a doorway opened back alongside the stairs. This passage opened into a room.

We still had no light. As we explored with our hands, I hit my knee against something hard and could not restrain a cry. Small rushed to my side, bumping into the thing himself and letting out an identical cry. We felt a low table before us, with scrolls and fine paintbrushes. A backrest sat nearby.

We found nothing else in the room but two heavy

chests and another backrest. The walls had the smooth, dusty feel of a stucco painting. No tapestries hid other doors. No break in the stone floors led to deeper levels.

We returned through the passageway, checking again for any other openings. We followed the stairs up to the altar room.

The Temple of Ah Puch was empty. Smoke Shell was not there.

CHAPTER THIRTEEN

e could not refrain from running a little as we fled down the steps of that dismal mound of stone. I swore I would never go there again.

We crouched in a dark corner of the plaza, letting our breathing and pulses return to normal and our muscles relax.

"I have not been so frightened since the day you first saw me," I whispered.

"What now?"

"They could have him anywhere. Any of the temples, the palace—He must be in the palace, but we'll never get in there. Too many guards."

"I think I would fall dead if we try. Ask Mother?"

"Mother would kill me if she knew what I was doing."

We sat in silence. I studied the plaza, surrounded by the Temple of Chac, the god of rain; the Temple of Yam Kax, the young corn god; the Temple of Itzamna, the high god and creator of people; the Temple of Kinich Kakmo, the sun god; and the Temple of the

First Oracle, where King Flint Sky God would be buried, along with his human sacrifice.

I did not know where Smoke Shell was that night. But I knew where he would be in the morning.

I would go to the Temple of the First Oracle and wait.

We could see guards on either side of the temple door. The burial chamber had already been filled with the treasures that would accompany King Flint Sky God to the otherworld, and these guards would protect the tomb until it was sealed.

"You will have to distract them, so I can get inside," I said.

"How?"

"Go around to the side, there. Wait until I get to the bottom of the steps, then make some noise. Yell, or throw something. Get them to chase you for a while. But don't get caught!"

"I cannot follow you then."

"No. Go home. In the morning, tell Mother that I went for a walk because I was upset. I will find her at the burial ceremony." I smiled, trying to be brave. "And I will have Smoke Shell with me!"

Small crept off around the temple, and the tree-stones now hid me as I darted from one to another until I could slip into my place, out of sight at the bottom of the temple steps, prepared to run. I heard a wailing that made the hair rise on my neck. It took me a moment to realize that the terrible noise must be Small. He sounded like a dozen night demons in agony.

The guards lifted their spears in a panic. Two more rushed out of the temple. I hadn't thought about others inside. I heard them whispering above me, their four voices mingled.

"What is that?"

"Evil spirits!"

"Come to torment the king?"

"It could be a trick."

"We have to investigate."

"You go."

"I'm not going out there. You go."

I hoped Small had not done too good a job. But the guards finally decided that three of them would go together to confront the noise. The last stayed behind to guard the temple, but he left the doorway to peer over the low wall along the stairs, where he could watch his comrades meet their fate.

I slipped up the steps, keeping to the opposite wall, as the wailing drifted into the distance, stopping and then beginning again from a different direction. The fourth guard was still turned away from me. I hesitated at the doorway, then plunged through it.

The front room was empty except for torches, the remnants of dinner and a gambling game, and the painted figures dancing across the walls. I could no longer hear Small's wailing, and the guards could return at any moment. The stairway before me led down into blackness. I picked up a spare torch and lit it from one in a wall sconce, hoping they would not notice the loss.

"What was it?" I heard the fourth guard yell.

I dashed down the stairs, desperate to get out of sight before the guards returned to see my light.

The stairs were long and steep. When I had almost reached the bottom, my foot shot off one of the narrow steps, and I landed hard on one hip and elbow, the torch spinning through the air and landing at the base of the stairway, sputtering.

I forced myself to ignore the pain and limp down to retrieve the torch before it expired. I could not stand another hour in an unfamiliar temple with nothing to light my way.

I coaxed the flame into fullness, then dashed away from the doorway as I heard the guards' voices in the room above. Pressed into a corner and shielding the light with my body, I finally had a chance to look around.

I was in the burial chamber. A small room, deep inside the temple. This chamber had been chosen and many of the burial items prepared years ago, when the king first became sick, or even earlier. It takes a long time to bury a king properly.

The stone coffin rested on massive chiseled blocks, almost filling the room. It was covered with beautiful carvings and painted red inside, the color of death. A massive stone slab lay against the wall, ready to cover the top. The king would be buried wearing his richest jewels: gold and jade forming his headdress, ear plugs, bead collar, breastplate, bracelets, rings, and sandals. He would carry a jade bead in his mouth, so he could buy food in the otherworld.

The walls were lined with clay jugs and pots, some carved with designs, others painted in black and shades of orange with detailed scenes of gods and people in ceremonial activities. They held food and drink for the afterlife. I recognized some of the type my father brought home from a trip all the way to the kingdom of Palenque, far to the northwest.

Some of these delicate, shallow bowls held hundreds of pieces of shell or polished jade in wonderful colors—shiny metallic blue, mottled green and white, pale gray with charcoal streaks, nut brown, and pale pink, as well as the more popular shades of green. A larger dish held a dozen whole cocoa fruits, each so big it would take both my hands to encircle one of the orange spheres. Another bowl was piled with red, orange, and green peppers, delicate and slender like curved fingers.

A large urn was modeled to resemble the grotesque face of a god. Incense burners painted or etched with delicate images held balls of resin. Six life-size heads modeled in stucco sat in niches in the walls, which were painted with scenes of the journey to the otherworld.

On the left wall, a canoe was paddled by the Old Jaguar God in front and the Ancient Stingray Spine God behind. Five passengers sat between them: a dog, a parrot, King Flint Sky God, a spider monkey, and an iguana. Each held a wrist to his forehead, the signal of impending death. The symbols above the scene said, "King Flint Sky God canoed eighty-three years to his passing."

The right wall showed the canoe plunging into the water. The dog was already submerged, while the parrot struggled in the waves. The king, the monkey, and the iguana were still in the canoe with the stingray god.

The back wall had a wonderful picture of the world. The Cosmic Monster, a giant crocodile, was stretched across the wall, resting on the surface of a lily pond. The thirteen upperworlds floated above him, while the nine underworlds were suspended below, their people and gods upside down in the murky waters. The blue-green World Tree rose through each layer, its roots in the underworld, its branches in the upperworld. In the middleworld, the tree became King Flint Sky God, reaching to the heavens to commune with the gods.

As I studied this image in the pale light, I felt at peace. King Flint Sky God had been a good king, and

I would miss him. But he had gone to live in the otherworld, with the gods. Future kings could commune with him through the World Tree when they practiced the acts of bloodletting and sacrifice. Death was the way of the world, like the change of the seasons and the rising of the sun.

But Great Skull Zero had disrupted the patterns of life. He acted for his own glory, not that of the gods. He must not be allowed to become king.

I must have slept a little, for I didn't hear the great wailing from outside the temple until I also heard footsteps on the stairs and the priests chanting. The torch lay spent beside me in the gloom; I grabbed it and scrambled to a hiding place in the back corner, where I was hidden by the coffin and its stone lid.

My heart leaped as the first people entered. Smoke Shell was at the front of the procession, wearing the cloak Feather Dawn had made him. He helped carry the king, who was wrapped in a red cotton shroud and fitted with a jade mask, deep green like the jungle. Great Skull Zero held the opposite side of the pallet in front. The other sacrificial victims and priests followed behind.

They laid the king in the coffin. My turn had come. I stood up, only a few feet away from Smoke Shell.

He was facing the coffin and did not see me at first, but Great Skull Zero did.

I had prepared a speech, but my mind was frantic and I said the first thing that came to me.

"Great Skull Zero is wrong! The gods do not—"

Smoke Shell spun and let out a gasp of surprise, but before he could speak or act, Great Skull Zero stepped forward. He raised his staff and cut off my speech with a blow to my head. My brother's open mouth melted into black as I sank at his feet.

awoke in silence and darkness. When the pounding in my head had receded to a dull thud, I felt around me. I was still in the burial chamber. I steadied myself on the coffin as I rose. The stone slab now covered the top. Where had everyone gone?

I felt around me in the blackness until I found my torch. With the obsidian knife I had slipped in my waistband, I cut a piece of my skirt, wrapping it around the top of the wood and tucking the end under. Then I dipped my fingers into the clay pots and jugs around me, feeling corn, beans, shells, peppers, and finally oil. I dipped my torch into the small jug.

I found an incense burner nearby and with it some flint. After a few tries, I got enough of a spark to light the torch. I held it carefully until the flame licked over all the cloth. Finally I stood to look around me.

Light flickered over the king's sarcophagus, sealed with the stone lid painted red and carved with an image of the king falling down the World Tree. His royal jade belt lay across the lid.

In the shadows beyond the coffin, a massive stone block filled the entrance to the crypt. In front of it were six bodies wrapped in red shrouds.

I began to scream.

When I could stop sobbing, I picked myself up off the floor and retrieved the torch that threatened to light my hair on fire. I went to the bodies and knelt beside the one I knew, intuitively, was Smoke Shell.

I had failed.

I stroked his chest, my fingers turning red from the cinnabar ore sprinkled over him. Exhausted, I shifted to lie down beside him. A scrap of linen came loose from my waistband. I picked it up slowly. The writing on it was rough and blurred. It seemed to have been written in blood.

It said, "Courage, sister. I go willingly."

Smoke Shell's last message, meant to comfort me. He knew that sacrificial victims got lives of ease in the otherworld. And he thought he was doing what was right for his king and his people. He would be, in death as in life, a hero.

I tucked the cloth back into my skirt carefully. Great Skull Zero must have allowed that message, but surely Smoke Shell hadn't known I would be left in there. He must have been told that I would be removed before they closed the tomb.

Had they forgotten me? Had Great Skull Zero thought me dead? Or had he left me to die slowly?

I could no longer save Smoke Shell, but I would have to try to save myself. I knew I could never move the stone blocking the entrance. Anyway, the stairway would have been filled with rubble. Still, I pushed against it with all my force. Nothing.

The stones were cemented together with a lime-stone mortar that hardened to become as solid as the rocks themselves. Breaking straight out through a wall was impossible. Beyond this room I would only find rubble in every direction, piled to the top of the temple and held in place by occasional retaining walls. I could not get to the outer wall without the rubble above caving in on me, and if I somehow did, I would only find massive stones too big for me to move.

This tomb was meant to prevent anyone from breaking in to steal the treasures of the king. This also made it difficult for anyone to break out. I examined the room carefully. It was not entirely closed off; next to the door was an opening. This stone duct would run alongside the stairway to the top room, so the priests could call down and commune with the spirit of the king. I could put my arm into it, but little more.

Through the duct I could hear a faint wailing, the voices of a thousand mourners in the plaza. My mother would be among them.

I sank to the floor exhausted and suddenly hungry.

I hadn't eaten and had barely slept since the day before. With a prayer to King Flint Sky God begging him not to mind my intrusion, I rummaged through the pots and had a meal of peanuts and a banana. I washed it down with a few sips of balché. Then, feeling sick and dizzy, I curled up on the hard stone floor to sleep.

I awoke groggy, but my head cleared quickly when I remembered my horrible situation. I cut off another piece of my skirt, dipped it in oil, and attached it to the flickering torch. I guessed that I had enough food and light for a week or so, if I were willing to use all of the king's stores, which I hated to do. I must escape quickly or not at all.

With my obsidian knife I began to scratch at the seams between the limestone blocks around the communication duct. Limestone is not as hard as other stones, but the work was slow and hot. The torch used up much of the little air that came through the vent, and the limestone dust clogged my nose and throat.

I finally loosened one block, which was too heavy for me to lift. I had to slowly slide it out and down the wall. I sat on it to rest while I drank some water, then began the next one.

When the second stone came free, I had cleared an opening large enough for my shoulders. I began to work to the left, hoping to break into the stairwell. Although it would be filled with rubble, at least I

would only have to move the stones, not cut them out of their places first.

By the time I had access to the stairwell, which was indeed full of rubble, I was too sore to move any more stones. I wondered how long I had been working and whether it was day or night outside. I had no way of knowing.

I knew I would never get out of that temple on my own. My brother, whom I had loved more than anyone in the world, lay dead at my feet. Perhaps I should join him. I held my knife in my open hand. The blade was now worn and chipped, pale limestone dirt marring the shiny blackness, but it would still pierce my flesh easily. I closed my fingers around it.

A small voice inside me said, "No. Not yet."

I let my shaking arm drop to my side. While I could breathe, I would fight. And I would find a way to punish Great Skull Zero.

I prayed to Ix Chel for courage and stamina. In the silence, I thought I heard her call my name.

The voice spoke again, a low but distinct hiss.

"Eveningstar! Eveningstar, are you there?"

I turned to the communication duct. "Yes! I am here!"

There was a long pause. "Are you a spirit, or are you alive?" It was not a goddess who spoke, but my mother.

"I am alive. I'm trapped here."

"Small and I will get you out."

"I have broken through to the stairway, but it's filled with rubble."

"Not all the way. The workers heard screams from the tomb and were scared. But the rest will be done tomorrow. We must get you out tonight."

My heart soaring with hope, I went to work, piling chunks of limestone among the pots. Above me, others were working to save me, and that made all the difference.

I didn't try to clear the whole stairwell, just a strip along the side large enough for me to crawl through. I banged my head, scraped my knees and arms, scratched my hands until they bled, and choked on the dusty stale air, but still I worked with the thought of freedom ahead.

Finally, as I lay in the dark passage, reaching for another stone, the rubble ahead of me began to shift.

"Wait!" I yelled. "I'm just on the other side. Let me move back."

I inched backward out into the room then called out, "All right!"

I heard grunts and the clatter of shifting stones, then the magical sound of my mother's voice as dust and pebbles bounced down around me.

"Eveningstar?"

"Yes! I'm coming!"

I glanced around the burial chamber one last time.

"Dear King Flint Sky God. Forgive me for making such a mess of your tomb. I hope you will understand."

I knelt beside my brother.

"Smoke Shell. Rest peacefully." I could think of nothing else to say.

Making sure I still had Smoke Shell's last message tucked in my skirt, I wriggled through the narrow tunnel. Hands grabbed mine and pulled me. Then I was sitting in the stairwell, wrapped in my mother's arms, both of us crying.

Small stood nearby, his wide grin lighting up the darkness better than the torch he held.

At last Mother loosened her grip. She took my face in both her hands and looked at me.

"My darling daughter. You are very brave and very stupid."

I laughed.

"We have much still to do," she continued. "It is almost dawn."

They had cleared only one side of the stairwell, piling the rubble farther up the steps. We chose speed over stealth this time, tossing the stones back down the stairs. They rolled and bounced with echoing rumbles, but no one came.

Finally we had the rubble back in place. We ignored the dust and small stones that still littered the stairs and stepped into the top room to see four guards asleep, sprawled messily and snoring.

"I gave them some balché with a little extra something in it!" Mother informed me with a wink.

We stepped past them to see the plaza bathed in soft gray light. Dirty, bruised, and scratched, we hurried down the temple steps and through the streets under a soft drizzle, ignoring the startled looks on the faces of the few people who were already outside.

When we reached our house, we collapsed. Double Bird sat up in bed and stared at us.

"Eveningstar! Where have you been?"

None of us had the energy to answer. Mother was the first to stir. She brought me some water, then began to warm tortillas on the hearth. The smell woke my father, who got up grumbling.

"Oh, there you are," he said to me. Then he took a few tortillas and wandered out to the courtyard.

The rest of us ate wrapped in our own thoughts. When we finished, Mother rose stiffly.

"Let's get you cleaned up, little duck, and then you can sleep."

I nodded, but when I tried to rise, my legs wouldn't hold me. Small scrambled to his feet and helped me. I leaned on his arm and looked into his dirty, gentle face.

"Thank you," I said.

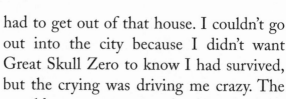had to get out of that house. I couldn't go out into the city because I didn't want Great Skull Zero to know I had survived, but the crying was driving me crazy. The whole city would go on mourning for days, weeping quietly during the day, wailing like blaring trumpets at night. I would have been angered and insulted had people gone about cheerfully as if nothing had happened, but I still couldn't take the racket, especially from Double Bird and Feather Dawn.

Double Bird's grief echoed in the emptiness of her eyes so that it hurt to look at her. I had not forgotten Smoke Shell's command that I take care of his wife, but time was all that could help her, and perhaps the birth of her baby. I didn't want to look at her sorrowful face; it reminded me too strongly that I could do nothing for her.

Feather's tears had the opposite effect. I hated her. I couldn't help it. She had done nothing to stop the sacrifice, nothing to comfort others. She lay paralyzed by her whimpering, acting as if she were the only one hurt. And she had not helped rescue me. I knew she had not been asked, but I blamed her all the same.

I could not bear to look at either of them, and the wailing that echoed in the streets raked my nerves like they were being rubbed across a grinding stone. Mother understood; I had done my mourning, trapped in a tomb with my brother's body, and I had been propelled forward with the struggle for my own life. I could not now go back into the comfort of grieving. I wanted to fight.

Mother suggested that I visit the surrounding villages, with Small as my companion. I would travel as a healer, taking medicine and bandages to treat any ill peasants. I had accompanied my mother on these journeys before, and I would be welcomed with food and a place to stay.

While I was there, Mother suggested in a low voice, I might see what the people thought of all that had happened. She did not elaborate, but I understood and my heart soared. We had not given up the fight. Perhaps people could be turned against Great Skull Zero, and Smoke Shell's death might be avenged.

The trip had an added bonus. If Great Skull Zero came looking for me, I would not be home.

My fourteenth birthday passed without ceremony during the second month of my travels. I had not planned to stay away for so long, but there was always one more town to visit, one more illness to treat, one more story to hear.

I had not realized how bad things were in the country. In the city, we had been told that food was plentiful. But the previous year had been dry and the crops small. The hunting had been worse, too, as animals moved away to lusher regions.

Yet royal messengers demanded more taxes than ever before, saying they were necessary to fill the storehouses. They told the peasants that everyone was suffering, that the nobles, too, were cutting back. I remembered the great feasts that had seemed to take place weekly in the previous year, some of which I had attended as a member of an honored family, and I blushed with shame.

I hadn't known! No one had known—though a few people, at least, must have. I asked about the messengers. They were priests and minor nobles, mostly. I recognized a few names. Curl Snout, the official at my Descent of the Gods ceremony, and other close associates of Great Skull Zero.

I remembered Great Skull Zero at many of those feasts, sitting beside the host, treating him like a brother, and showing him the favor of the gods, or hosting himself, and seeing that the most important men had the best delicacies and plenty of balché to drink.

The nobles had celebrated while the peasants

struggled. This was not the Mayan way. The priests, the nobles, and most of all the king were there to serve the people, to take care of them, guide them, and commune with the gods on their behalf, not to feast while others starved.

Now the situation was growing worse. Great Skull Zero had not yet declared himself king, but he was acting with all the power of kingship. He had ordered a new palace built for himself, plus three new temples to glorify the city, and the peasants would have to supply the workers. Every strong man was taken.

The villages had lost so many people in the War with the Savages and the accompanying disease that they needed everyone to prepare the fields for planting. Women and children were forced to take over the fields, turning the soil with heavy hoes made from stone blades lashed to sturdy sticks. They were not able to clear new land without more help, so they were forced to reuse land that was no longer fully fertile, and they couldn't maintain the irrigation channels.

A few weeks after my birthday, I was staying in a small village with a bony woman named Owl Scroll. Like most of the peasants Small and I had been staying with over the past few months, Owl Scroll lived in a small hut made of poles lashed together with vines and plastered with mud. We sat on the packed-earth floor, light filtering in through the thatched roof where it needed repairs. Her baby tried to suck a little milk from her thin breast, and her older children watched me with dark eyes, too tired to play or fuss. Like many of the children I had seen in the villages, they had the scabs, bruises, and bleeding gums that came from a poor diet, but I had given them the last of my dried chili powder and they seemed to be improving.

Owl Scroll spoke in a soft, shaky voice. "They took my husband, and my sisters' husbands, and my brothers. They wanted my oldest son, but I swore he was not yet a man. They left only the children and my father, who is lame. We all must work in the fields now. The corn must be planted after the next moon."

She looked at me desperately. "Surely they will send the men home then." Her face did not echo the certainty of her words. "We cannot do it without them."

Her father leaned forward from a dark corner and tapped his walking stick on the floor near me. His voice was much stronger than his crooked, frail body.

"You nobles think you can take the best land and put your houses there," he said. "Ever since I was a boy, you've been sweeping aside the farmers for that city, and then you want more food for all those people there."

Owl Scroll blushed.

"Father! Eveningstar is our guest." She turned to me. "We don't hate the city, really. We need the king and the priests to talk to the gods for us and to make sure the gods don't get angry. And we need the warriors to protect us. We don't mind paying taxes and sending workers for building. We've always done our part. But the wars were hard on us. We lost so many—"

Her father broke in again. "There are more nobles than farmers now. All the best young people want to go to the city, learn a trade, work their way up, and start wearing fancy jewelry and nice clothes. And since your brother rose so high from a merchant family, everyone thinks they can move up the ranks, too. But somebody has to grow the food. Lose respect for the land and the people who work it, and you won't survive for long. They'll see now."

My head was pounding with all they had told me. I felt ashamed of the jade in my ears and around my neck. We had been so proud of our rise in status, thinking we were better than we had been before, when really we were no better than these poor farmers, and in some ways maybe worse.

"What can be done?" I asked.

"That high priest must send the men home," Owl Scroll said. "Or we will starve."

The old man laughed. He sounded almost satisfied. "And the rest of you with us."

Small and I helped Owl Scroll and her family in the fields the next day, turning the hard dry earth with stone hoes until my arms and back ached. At the end of the day, I looked back at what I had done, and it seemed so little. Yet I could barely lift a spoon to my lips, let alone help Owl Scroll make the stew. I was famished, but we had barely enough food to take the edge off the hunger. Owl Scroll would have given me a little extra, but I insisted it go to the children.

In the morning, I could hardly move my arms. Small insisted that I could do more good with my medicine. I knew he was right, but the aching muscles could not cover my guilt. Instead, knowing just how hard these people worked, I felt even worse.

I gave Owl Scroll some snakeroot for the children's stomach pains, and her father some palm nuts to help his blood flow, then Small and I continued on our travels.

Horrible rumors began to reach us.

Nobles were being sacrificed.

Not war captives, but our own people, men and women, adults and children, were being thrown into the Well of Sacrifice. Some said hundreds or even thousands of people had died. Others said, no, not so many, but the victims were often members of the best and most powerful families. They were given the task of asking the gods for the name of the next king, but no one had yet survived to bring back a message. Why, the people wondered, had the gods grown so angry?

With a sense of dread, I thought of my family. The time had come to return to the city. I hated to leave the peasants in such a terrible state, but I had done all I could alone.

mall and I traveled for a day and a half to reach the city, arriving on the day Four Net. It was a day for paying debts, not the best day for returning home when danger awaited, but the following day would be even worse, Five Snake, a day that brings an enemy. And I didn't want to wait beyond that. We decided to stay at the edge of the jungle until nightfall. Feeling restless and anxious, I began to search for medicinal plants, just for something to do. My supplies were gone, anyway.

Small wandered down along the river, probably to visit the grave of his companions. By the time he returned, dusk was settling and I had started a small fire for light and friendship. I had found some wild tomatoes and jicama to go with the handful of corn we had for dinner, plus some medicinal roots. Small brought back a handful of fat, pale grubs, the kind found in rotting palm logs, thicker than his thumb and twice as long. They were not my favorite food, but after two months of little but corn, they added a nice richness to the stew.

We ate in silence, with frequent glances in the direction of the city, even though we couldn't see it through the trees and darkness. The fire died down to glowing embers. Farther in the jungle, a jaguar called out in a short booming cough and was answered by another. I drew my shawl more snugly around my shoulders, feeling a shiver despite the warm air of the dry season.

Small's dark eyes watched me across the fire. He rose and slid through the darkness as gracefully as a jungle cat. At my side he unrolled a blanket and we wrapped it around ourselves, sitting shoulder to shoulder and hip to hip. I realized how useful Small had been to me during our travels. I had come to depend on him, not just for physical help, but for understanding and support. I enjoyed his company, and in many ways I knew him better than I had ever known any man, even Smoke Shell or my father. The worse things got, the happier I was to have Small near me.

His features were just visible in the shadows. I no longer noticed how different he was from the Mayan men, with his flatter, rounder face and lighter skin. He had grown a little since we first met, I realized suddenly, and his chest and limbs were muscular. Small was no longer a proper description for him.

When I saw a faint silver glow from the moon through the trees, I took a deep breath and turned to Small. "It is time," I said softly.

He rose wordlessly and held out his hand. I didn't need help getting up, as he must have known, but I took his hand and the warmth of his fingers was comforting.

We walked close together through the deserted farmlands, the silhouettes of the temples ahead rising black against the deep blue sky. A few lights flickered in the city, but the streets were quiet, and we passed by the farmers' mud-and-thatch huts, through the neighborhood of the wealthy merchants and professionals, and into the area reserved for nobles, without attracting notice.

I paused outside our house, its limestone walls glowing eerily. Soft voices came from within. With Small at my heels, I quietly climbed the steps and drew aside the hanging in the doorway.

Double Bird saw us first and let out a small shriek.

"It's all right," I said, stepping inside quickly. "It's just me."

Mother rose and embraced me.

"Thank Ix Chel," she said. "I was worried about you."

"I'm fine. But things are terrible in the villages. And we've heard rumors."

"Yes, the sacrifices. Come sit. Small, welcome back. Thank you for watching over my daughter."

Mother bustled about, making us some atole, a thick, hot drink of cornmeal and honey. Double Bird sat cross-legged, her swollen belly filling her lap like a cooking pot, and watched us, as did Feather Dawn, lounging on a reed mat.

"Where is Father?" I said, suddenly worried.

"He's on a trading trip," Mother replied, handing Small and me each a clay cup of atole. "Pray he doesn't come back soon."

"Why?"

The room was suddenly somber. Mother led me to a mat, exchanging glances with Double Bird and Feather Dawn.

"Great Skull Zero wants to marry your sister."

Feather sat up a little prouder as I stared at her.

"You won't!"

"Of course not," Mother said. "As long as your father is away, we can put off his requests. But it is difficult to refuse outright. Many people have died for less."

"So it's true, about the sacrifices?"

"Great Skull Zero is eliminating all opposition. He's pious about it, claiming the will of the gods and telling his victims to ask the gods for the name of the next king, as if he weren't planning on being king himself."

"No one has survived the Well of Sacrifice yet?"

"No one. That rarely happens anyway, but I suspect Great Skull Zero would finish off any survivors before they could speak against him."

"Why hasn't he declared himself king yet?" I asked.

"He is maintaining the pretense of doing the gods' will. Many people are still afraid to argue. And if the wrath of the gods doesn't scare them, fear of the Well of Sacrifice will. Soon there will be no one left strong enough to oppose him. Already he has eliminated anyone who might have made a good king. Even if we could get rid of Great Skull Zero, I don't know who would replace him."

"How long can he continue?"

"I don't think he'll need much longer. The nobles have met several times to choose a new king, but as soon as they name someone, Great Skull Zero announces that the candidate is to be sacrificed. Now no one wants to be chosen. But becoming king is not a simple matter of donning a royal headdress. Even legitimate princes may take years to ascend the throne. The people want stability. Great Skull Zero must prove not only that he has power but that his dynasty will last."

"So he needs a son."

"Yes. He divorced his first wife years ago because they had no children. His current wife was pregnant once, but the child was sickly and soon died. So he will take another."

"But why Feather? How can he think she would be willing after what he has done?"

"Great Skull Zero thought that killing Smoke Shell would erase him, but he was wrong. Smoke Shell is more of a hero now than he was alive, for going so bravely to his death at the command of the gods. Great Skull Zero wants your sister because marrying into Smoke Shell's family will give his bid for the crown legitimacy."

"That's not the only reason," Feather said petulantly.

"And because your sister is so beautiful and talent-ed," Mother added with a smile.

"Great Skull Zero will not wait forever," I said.

"No. We must leave the city."

"Just leave? Give up?"

Mother leaned over and took my hand. "Dear, brave daughter. We have no choice. People are unhap-py, but they are still too afraid to rebel. We would need a strong leader, and none are left."

"I could rule better than Great Skull Zero," I said grumpily.

Mother grinned with affection. "True. The first being in creation crowned as king was Lady Beastie, the First Mother. A few queens have ruled after their husbands died and before their sons were old enough. Some were great rulers and much respected. But that is a different situation. I don't think people would fol-low a woman outside the royal family, especially one so young."

"I wish I were a man."

"If you were a man, you would already be dead," Mother replied.

◆◆◆

We talked late into the night, discussing plans. The best option seemed to be to leave as soon as Double Bird's baby was born, hopefully within the week. Double Bird wanted to come with us, but Mother thought she should stay with her family. I would have to remain in hiding until we were ready to go.

I slept late the next morning, exhausted from my travels and finally sated by the food Mother had pressed on me the night before. I was dressing, leaning out a little from behind the sleeping partition to speak with Double Bird, when our door hanging was swept back suddenly.

Silhouetted against the sunny street was Great Skull Zero.

I jumped back, pressing myself against the partition, my heart beating like the frenzied drums during a sacrifice. A wave of nausea swept over me, and my knees buckled at the memory of waking in the tomb to find my brother's dead body.

Double Bird screamed, and my mother said, "What do you want here?"

His voice was cold and precise, with an evil smile in it. "Eighteen Rabbit is back."

The room was silent as we considered the news. My father, not knowing the trouble we were in, had not bothered to come into the city secretly. He had brought his canoe up to the main dock, right by the marketplace, and had probably begun unloading his goods and cheerfully gossiping with his friends.

"We will go to see him now," Great Skull Zero continued. "You will advise him to give your daughter to me in marriage."

"Never."

"You will do as I say," Great Skull Zero said coldly. "Or you will have no children left at all."

"Very well," Mother answered softly. "As soon as Eighteen Rabbit comes home, we shall discuss the matter. We will come to the palace with our answer."

"You will come now!" Great Skull Zero roared.

"Let go of her!" Mother yelled, as Feather Dawn and Double Bird screamed.

I looked around the corner to see Great Skull Zero holding Feather by her hair and raising a hand to strike Mother as she rushed forward.

"No!" I yelled, or perhaps I only made some unintelligible sound, as I threw myself at Great Skull Zero, beating at him with my small fists.

His surprise interrupted his swing at Mother, but my victory was short. Without letting go of Feather's hair, he grabbed me with his free hand and flung me against the wall behind him. A throbbing rang through my shoulder and arm where I hit, and I collapsed on the ground, stunned. I felt Mother's arms close around me.

"So you are alive," Great Skull Zero said. "I had heard rumors. Guards!"

Two warriors holding wooden war clubs pushed through the narrow doorway while two others with stone-tipped spears peered in from outside.

"Take this girl away. She has been chosen as a messenger to the gods."

Screams and moans filled the room as one of the guards struggled to extract me from Mother's embrace. Small jumped up and swung a ceramic bowl at the guard. The guard's headdress broke the swing and the bowl, sending pottery shards flying. The second guard quickly stepped forward and smashed his war club against the side of Small's head. Small crumpled to the floor, his eyes closed and his hair glistening with blood.

The first guard recovered, grabbed me around the waist, and lifted me, dragging Mother with us until the second guard roughly pried her off and pushed her to the floor. Great Skull Zero pulled Feather to her feet by her hair as Double Bird sobbed and rocked where she sat, clutching her stomach.

Great Skull Zero switched his grip to Feather's arm and guided her out of the house. The guard tossed me over his shoulder and followed. As they stomped up the street, I ignored the curious stares of passersby and gazed at the home I might never see again, listening to Mother's wails until they faded behind us.

 awoke to the sounds of screams and realized they were my own. I sat up, gasping for breath, and the blanket fell from my bare skin. My hands were shaking. They seemed so fragile in the dim light.

A lean face peered in the doorway, and I gathered the blanket to cover myself. The expressionless guard receded, letting the curtain fall back into place.

I listened carefully, trying to guess the time. I could not see the moon; the thick rock walls of the room prevented any natural light from entering. But there were other signs, the faint sounds of singing beetles and night birds that filtered through the stone corridors of the palace, my prison.

I decided that dawn must be near. No point trying to sleep. Soon, I would never sleep again—at least not in this world. I knelt on the fur-covered stone platform that had been my bed for the last three days. The thick, golden puma skins were an unaccustomed luxury, but I longed for my simple mat on the floor, with the smell of a fire and the varied sounds of breathing from my family.

I asked Ix Chel to bless my family, to protect my parents and sister, and to be merciful to my brother. When I had prayed for my family, I began to pray for myself. I hadn't the proper offerings, but Mother often said that Ix Chel would always listen, if you spoke with an open heart. I opened my heart to her then, that she might comfort and guide me in the terrible days ahead.

My meditations were interrupted by loud footsteps in the corridor. I could always recognize the high priest's steps. His sandals were decorated with beads of jade and gold, making them heavy like his large body. So when Great Skull Zero walked, it sounded as if someone were beating a drum, accompanied by a faint jingling from his many bracelets, his headdress, and the beads on his breastplate. It was a fearsome kind of music, though, with no joy or peace in it.

I noticed a faint band of light under the curtain at the door; it must indeed be day. The curtain was pulled aside roughly and a dark figure filled the doorway. I could not make out his face, but I recognized the heavy silhouette of Great Skull Zero. He stepped just inside the room, holding the curtain back to let in light.

"Good morning," he said, with a smile that showed all his remaining teeth. I forced myself not to shudder or look away. "One more day," he said. "Are you excited?"

"I know what day it is." It is supposed to be a great honor to be chosen as a sacrificial victim, a messenger to the gods. I did not feel honored.

Great Skull Zero tossed me some clothes. He had no illusions about my willingness, and sending me to bed naked was one of his little tricks to ensure I would not try to overpower the guard who was twice my size, break through the guards always stationed at the entrance of the palace complex, and slip out of the city to starve to death or be eaten by jaguars in the jungle.

"Hurry. We have much to do." He left the room and let the curtain fall. I heard his footsteps echoing down the corridor, for what he had to do and what I had to do were different things, and I would probably not see him until the next morning, when I would see him for the last time. He would lift me high over the Well of Sacrifice, then watch me plunge to the surface of the water far below.

If I survived, I was to ask the gods for the name of the next king. Great Skull Zero would not want me to survive.

I wrapped the skirt around my hips and fastened the shawl about my shoulders. They were of fine cotton, expertly woven, white with thin stripes the color

153

of dried blood and delicate embroidery at the edges. I wondered if my sister might have woven them. To keep my hair back, I merely took the waist-length mass and tied it in one large knot at the base of my skull. That would do for the moment. I was not trying to impress anyone.

When I left the room, the unsmiling, unspeaking guard began to walk, and I followed him. I paused at the top of the steps that led down into the courtyard, my eyes hungry for the view of the city. Across the courtyard, Great Skull Zero had begun building another palace, to be more grand than this or any other. The farmers, who should have been planting their corn, were already at work moving stones as the sun crept above the horizon, casting long shadows across the plaza.

They quarried the stones outside the city, dragging the pieces back on log rollers for the masons to cut and shape using stone tools. They had built a grid of low retaining walls, and they were filling those compartments with rubble before building higher. Some workers were burning pieces of limestone to a powder and mixing it with water to make the mortar that held the blocks together and the plaster for smoothing the walls. One day in the future, the facades and sloped roof would be covered with sculpture molded from a rich mix of plaster that dried to become as hard as stone. Temples and palaces were massive, solid constructions that took a great deal of time and strength.

Beyond the rubble of construction rose temples, the observatory, and the grand homes of nobles. I could not see my family's home among them, but I knew where it was, just out of sight behind the Temple of Chac. Farther out were the smaller homes of the merchants and professionals. Peasant huts dotted the distance, the smoke from their fires hazy in the cool morning air. The forest in the distance was the color of bone, many of the trees bare and bleached from the long dry season.

The guard turned at the bottom of the steps and grunted at me, annoyed at my dawdling. As I joined him, I lifted my chin a little higher and glared at him with what I hoped was a look of haughty pride. We continued across the plaza, past the tree-stones erected by generations of kings, plus a new one in progress that Great Skull Zero was having carved with his own image. It lay on its back, stretched across the plaza so the artists could finish the carving before hauling it upright. The bottom fourth was blank; it would extend into the ground to hold the monument in place for eternity.

We went to the Temple of Itzamna, the god of gods and creator of people, patron of science and learning, books and writing. Smoke Shell had studied there. The temple door was flanked by Itzamna masks, showing him as an old man with a large hooked nose and hollow cheeks over his toothless jaws. Above these images the god was depicted as a two-headed snake monster with bulging, square eyes.

The guard sat at the top of the steps to wait while I passed through the first room of the temple and glanced at the murals showing Itzamna in his embodiments as day and night, earth and sky.

I stopped in the doorway of the back room. The priest Smoking Squirrel, who had told me the story of the Hero Twins, turned his crooked body stiffly and gave me a sad, lopsided smile.

"Hello, child," he said softly.

I was no longer a child, but instead of offending, his words broke through my mask of pride and left me feeling terribly young and scared. I ran to him and buried my face in his chest, crying with choked sobs as he rocked me gently.

"I have seen your mother," he said at last.

I looked up at him with tear-stained cheeks. "How is she?" I asked, aching for her.

"Worried about you. But Double Bird had her baby, and he eases their pain a little."

"She had a boy," I said, feeling a surprising happiness.

"Born the day you were taken. The fright must have set off the birth. She named him Smoke Shell."

"I wish I could see him." The loneliness threatened to overwhelm me again.

"Perhaps you will," Smoking Squirrel said gently. He released me and moved stiffly to the table, picking up a book. "Now, my dear, we must prepare you for your mission."

"You know it's not really for the gods."

He seemed to crumple, his crooked back twisting in on itself and his face sagging.

"Yes." He forced himself to straighten. "But that is no reason to send you unprepared. Why you reach the otherworld is not so important as how the gods receive you. The proper rites of purification and fasting for a sacrifice take sixty days. Great Skull Zero will not give you that much time, but we must do what we can." He smiled bitterly. "I have had too much experience lately in preparing people to meet their fate before they are ready."

"Have we really been so evil to deserve such punishment?"

"Not intentionally, no. But we have been careless. The upper classes have grown, with more and more nobles demanding food and riches they have done very little to earn. And we have used up the land. I don't see how the city can survive much longer. King Flint Sky God knew we were in trouble, but he saw no answer. How do you tell rich lords that they must go without or, worse, that they must work in the fields? How do you cause trees to grow where the land has been stripped bare?"

"But why do the gods allow such things?"

Smoking Squirrel sighed. "Sometimes I think the gods do not pay nearly as much attention to us as we would like to think."

"You mean they don't care?"

"Not that, but rather . . ." He pondered a moment. "I think they leave us to make our own decisions and to suffer the consequences. Like a good parent who gives her child freedom so that he may grow strong and learn from his mistakes. The question is, are we learning? Or will we simply destroy ourselves?"

He opened the book, which was made of a long strip of bark paper folded like a screen, and spread out several pages on the table. I stood beside him and studied the delicate symbols, painstakingly painted in vivid colors with a fine brush.

"This is a prophecy written years ago," Smoking Squirrel said, running a bony finger down one page as he read, top to bottom. I didn't bother to read along, just watched his gentle old face, with cheeks sunken like Itzamna's, as he spoke.

Eat, eat, you have bread
Drink, drink, you have water
On that day, dust possesses the earth
On that day, a blight is on the face of the earth
On that day, a cloud rises
On that day, a mountain rises

159

On that day, a strong man seizes the land
On that day, things fall to ruin
On that day, the tender leaf is destroyed
On that day, the dying eyes are closed
On that day, three signs are on the tree
On that day, three generations hang there
On that day, the battle flag is raised
And they are scattered afar in the forests

"Scattered in the forests," I repeated slowly. "Do you think that prophecy is coming true now?"

"I don't know. We are in a very troubled time, but not all the signs are here. Prophecies are often confusing. Most of the leaves have been destroyed, dust is possessing the earth, and many dying eyes have closed. Our society is falling to ruin, if not the actual buildings of the city. But the strong man who seizes the land, is that Great Skull Zero, or another to come? What is the mountain that rises? Where are the signs on the tree? So far, we have raised no battle flag. Perhaps the prophecy speaks of an event far in the future."

"I guess it doesn't really give us any advice, anyway. Not much use knowing disaster is coming if you can't prevent it."

He smiled and patted my arm. "You are a wonderfully practical girl. Yes, I have heard what you did trying to save your brother."

"I failed, though, nearly died, and put myself and my family in more danger. I told you I act without thinking."

"That is better than to think without acting. We could use some action now." He stepped to the doorway and checked that the front room was empty. The guard still sat on the steps outside, gazing into space. Smoking Squirrel came back to me, leaned close, and whispered.

"You have had some time to think these last few days. Have any ideas come to you?"

"Ideas?" I stared at him in confusion, and he stared back intently. "You mean to escape?" I asked with surprise, then realized I had not lowered my voice. "I don't see how," I whispered. "They have guards everywhere at night."

Smoking Squirrel nodded sadly. "Yes. I suppose it is too much to ask. But know that I will help you in any way that I can."

"You will go against the high priest?"

"Great Skull Zero is wrong. And I would not be much of a priest if I lacked the courage that you showed as a mere girl. I would speak out, if it would do any good. . . ."

"But you would just lose your life as well."

"Yes. And then I could not help other poor souls who face their deaths. I have spoken in private when I could, encouraging people to question

161

Great Skull Zero's actions. I know a few who might help us."

"Oh, surely there is something we could do!" Just knowing that others were on my side gave me hope, although I still could see no way to escape.

"You are too well guarded at night, and those guards are loyal to Great Skull Zero. So you must escape during the day. And you are to go to the Well of Sacrifice tomorrow, so you must escape today."

"That doesn't leave us much time," I said doubtfully.

"This temple has only the one entrance."

"And the guard is waiting for me outside."

"So we must get rid of the guard and get you across the plaza and out of the city without attracting notice."

"Mother gave the guards at the Temple of the First Oracle some sort of drug in their drink."

"Hmm, yes. I have something that might work. A drug I use to help sick patients—and nervous sacrificial victims—sleep. It works slowly, though."

"They must not know that you had anything to do with this. You'll be needed here."

"I'll tell them the guard got drunk on duty. Great Skull Zero won't believe me, but he can hardly go around throwing respected old priests into the Well of Sacrifice without a very good reason."

"Will he drink it? He might be suspicious."

"He will if we ask right. But how to get you across the plaza unnoticed?"

I looked at the back of the guard sitting outside. I felt a smile creep across my face.

"He's small for a guard," I said.

moking Squirrel solemnly asked the guard to come inside. I tried to look sad, staring at the floor so he couldn't see my shining eyes.

"We are about to perform the Drink to the Spirits ritual," Smoking Squirrel said. I stifled a tense giggle.

"I've never heard of that one," the guard answered.

Smoking Squirrel eyed him coolly. "No. Unless you have been about to be sacrificed, I doubt you have."

"Oh!" The guard shuffled awkwardly, fumbling with his spear.

"The ritual requires three participants," Smoking Squirrel continued. "Since you are here, perhaps you could help us."

"But I'm not a priest or anything."

"You don't have to be. All you have to do is drink a cup of this honey mead and say 'If it pleases Itzamna' when I have finished the prayer."

"Mead, you say! I can do that."

"Very good. Let us begin."

Smoking Squirrel went to the table and picked up

a decorated clay jug of alcohol. He poured the sweet mead into three red-clay ritual cups and then passed them around. One of the cups had a large dose of sleeping potion already inside it, and that one the guard received.

We stood facing each other like three points of a triangle as Smoking Squirrel recited a rambling prayer, calling on the spirits to watch over me. When he finished, he looked at the guard expectantly.

"Oh! Uh, if it pleases Itzamna."

Smoking Squirrel nodded solemnly and lifted the cup. We all drank deeply, finishing the draught before removing the cups from our lips.

"Thank you," Smoking Squirrel said as he took the guard's cup. "You have been very helpful."

"I'll just wait outside, then," he answered, nodding to me with a sympathetic smile.

The priest and I waited anxiously for the potion to take effect as the sun rose high overhead.

"What will you do once you are out of the city?" Smoking Squirrel asked with worry.

I thought for a while. "I must contact my parents, I suppose, somehow."

"I can take a message to your mother."

"Perfect. Tell them I'll go to the place where Smoke Shell killed the first Savages. Small knows the way." My mind flew to the scene of Small crumpling to the floor after the war club hit his head. "I hope he's all right."

"Your slave? I've seen him. He has recovered, although he isn't talking or eating much."

"Dear Small. He has done so much for me. He can come to me by the river with a message. Or perhaps the whole family will come. They had talked about leaving, to protect Feather Dawn and me."

Smoking Squirrel bit his lip, looking concerned. "Your sister is to marry Great Skull Zero tomorrow."

"She can't!"

"She has no choice. Great Skull Zero threatened to throw Feather into the Well of Sacrifice."

"Better than marrying that monster!"

"He said he would send Double Bird's baby after her."

"He wouldn't!"

"You know he would. It is unusual to sacrifice a baby of noble standing, but Great Skull Zero has already broken many rules. I expect he'll try to find a way to get rid of the child anyway within a few years. He would not want Smoke Shell's son to grow old enough to take his revenge."

"You must tell my parents! Double Bird and her baby must leave with us."

"Yes. Your father is known in the coastal cities, and news of our city's trouble must have reached them by now. You will surely be welcomed there."

Our attention was caught by the guard outside. He had been letting his head drop to his chest, then jerking it up repeatedly. Now he slumped over on his side, his limp hand dropping the spear.

"Quickly!" Smoking Squirrel hissed.

We dashed outside, crouching down to stay out of view of the plaza below. Each of us grabbed an arm of the guard and dragged him roughly back into the temple. Panting, Smoking Squirrel pulled off the guard's cloak and headdress while I slipped off my skirt and shawl. I was soon dressed in the loose costume of the guard.

Smoking Squirrel grinned at me. "Well, you won't fool anyone close up, but keep your head down and move like you know what you're doing." He clasped my hand. "Good luck."

"Thank you," I said, leaning in to kiss his cheek.

I stepped firmly out of the temple, stooped to retrieve the spear lying on the steps, and marched down to the plaza with my heart pounding. I had not thought about which way I should go and frantically tried to decide on the safest route. Much as I wanted to see my family, I decided to avoid my home and Double Bird's family home, keeping to neighborhoods where no one should know me.

I quickly made my way out of the plaza and into a neighborhood populated by rich priests. The streets were broad, but few shadows offered protection at this time of day. I went several blocks without incident, but then a group of young women approached and I began to sweat. When I saw among them Dark House and Many Hands, who had been at our party several years before and had become friends of mine, I panicked and turned down a side street. I had not gone far when I saw a group of warriors. Surely they would notice that I was not really one of them. I took a few erratic steps before noticing an alley and slipping down it.

I followed the narrow street until I came out on a main street again. People seemed to be everywhere, chatting in small groups as they walked or hurrying alone looking worried. Thousands of people lived in the city, and I was shocked at how many I recognized. I had met so many people in my short life: my brother's and sister's friends, my mother's patients, my father's fellow traders, nobles and priests.

I kept turning down side streets to get away from people I knew. When forced to pass someone, I bowed my head as if in respect and walked briskly, as if I had important business waiting. If someone drew too close or seemed ready to look at me, I knelt and pretended I had a stone in my sandal.

My stomach churned and my shoulders knotted, but most people hardly glanced at me. I began to relax a little and tried to figure out how far I had to go. I recognized nothing.

I was lost.

The sun was high overhead, giving no indication of

the directions. I was still among the noble houses built on high platforms, which prevented me from seeing the looming temples of the city center.

I would have to keep going until I found something I recognized. I seemed to pass through endless streets, turning at random and getting nowhere. I couldn't tell if the sun was actually moving in one direction or if it just looked that way because I was changing my viewpoint. Strands of hair stuck to my face and the guard's loincloth was starting to slip down my hips. Finally I realized that if I just went straight in one direction I must eventually reach the edge of the city somewhere. The route might not be the shortest one, but it was better than going in circles.

I chose a street that was long and straight, but narrow and not very crowded. I marched as if I owned the street, looking straight ahead when forced to pass people. I soon came to the end.

Looking around the corner, I saw the Temple of the First Oracle. I had returned to the plaza.

My legs went weak for a moment, and I thought I could not possibly go through all that again. But I soon realized that all I had to do was turn around and walk in the opposite direction.

I gathered up my courage. Then I heard voices behind me, and without thinking, I turned.

Great Skull Zero rounded the corner, holding Feather Dawn by the arm and followed by two guards.

My whole body went numb, and I could neither move nor breathe. The high priest's eyes swept past me without pause and he kept walking. Trembling, I started to turn away.

Then Feather screamed.

"Eveningstar!" she shouted, breaking free from Great Skull Zero's grasp and lunging toward me. "Eveningstar, help me!"

Great Skull Zero spun with a bellow of rage. I tried to shake off Feather and run, but she clung to me, babbling in desperation.

"Grab her!" Great Skull Zero yelled. "Grab them both!"

The guards closed in on us and I was a captive once more. The sobbing Feather was returned to the high priest. He glared at me, and the hate in his eyes gave me a strange kind of courage. I looked at him without flinching.

"So, Eveningstar Macaw," he spat. "You have become a warrior. Interesting. But it will not save you from the Well of Sacrifice."

He turned and stomped off, dragging Feather, who gasped plaintively, "Please, Eveningstar, help me!"

My silly sister had never paid any attention to me before. She had to choose this day, I thought angrily, as the guards holding my arms pulled me across the plaza.

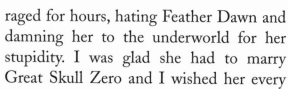raged for hours, hating Feather Dawn and damning her to the underworld for her stupidity. I was glad she had to marry Great Skull Zero and I wished her every misery. She deserved it. She hadn't the courage or imagination to save herself, so she had to drag me down with her.

What could she possibly have thought I would do, knock down Great Skull Zero and two guards with a slap and carry her off to safety? In the stolen guard's clothes, I thought with bitter humor, she had mistaken me for Smoke Shell. If only he were alive, we might have some hope. But then Smoke Shell hadn't even saved himself.

Finally, exhausted, I lay back on the puma skins in my tiny cell and stared at the whitewashed ceiling. Mother's words came back to me. She is not as strong as you. Feather was weak and foolish, but more than that, she was scared. This was the first serious confrontation in her easy life, and she saw no escape. I should have been flattered, in fact, that she thought me capable of helping her, even if her sudden belief in me was a result of panic.

Feather had been the one flaw in my escape plan all along. Our parents would not leave without her. If they could not prevent her marriage to the high priest, they would at least stay to offer what support and comfort they could. They would send me on with Double Bird and her baby, but we would no longer be a family.

Was this what my life had come to, that at fourteen I was responsible for saving not only myself, but my older sister, and even our whole family? I had not even been able to save Smoke Shell.

As my anger receded, a terrible fear and helplessness overcame me. The walls and ceiling seemed to close in on me, trapping me, pressing out my breath and life. With a stifled gasp I rolled over and buried my face in the furs, trying to block out the world. But not being able to see the ceiling only made me all the more certain that it was coming to crush me.

I sat up and backed into the corner, huddling with my arms wrapped around my knees. Desperately I searched for something to distract myself. I tried to get angry again; anger had been so much nicer than fear, but it was gone. Trying to picture Feather as she betrayed me only brought back the image of the high priest.

Great Skull Zero towering over me with evil in his

eyes. Great Skull Zero raising his staff to hit me in the burial chamber. Great Skull Zero wanting to see me dead.

I had been a fool to challenge him, the most powerful man in the kingdom now that the king was dead. I should never have gotten involved.

Then I thought of my brother. I had not been able to save him, but if I had not tried, I would have spent the rest of my life wishing I had done something—anything—to try. I could not have lived with the knowledge that I had just stood in the plaza and watched my brother walk to his death. If I could go back, I would not change my choices.

I noticed my chest heaving, and I tried to calm my breathing. The guards outside—two of them now—were eating their evening meal. No one had brought me anything. I didn't care; I couldn't have eaten. I was suddenly thirsty, though. I pulled the blanket up under my arms.

"Excuse me," I called out.

One of the guards pulled back the curtain and stuck his head in.

"Could I have some water, please?"

They grumbled among themselves, but one of them brought a gourd of water. I sipped from it as he settled himself back outside the door. Then I lay back, staring at the ceiling, tired and sick but unable to sleep. I tried to pray, but I couldn't focus even on that, so I just asked Ix Chel to comfort me and tried to empty my mind altogether.

Sometime later I heard the guards talking.

"I have to go to the bathroom."

"So go, already."

"I'll be right back. Be careful."

"Oh, come on. It's just a girl."

"She's a slippery one. She got away before. Twice, if you believe that rumor about her being trapped in the king's burial room."

"That's impossible. And she only got away today because she had help and that idiot Spearthrower Boar wasn't doing his job. He'll be lucky if he doesn't lose his head."

"She tricked him. That's why you have to be careful."

"I won't even talk to her."

There was a rustle and a faint gleam of lantern light as he pulled back the curtain.

"She's asleep, anyway. Just go."

I heard footsteps pad off down the hallway. A sudden thought entered my mind.

This is your last chance.

I slipped out of bed and lifted the half-full water gourd, feeling its weight. I crept to the curtain, not daring to breathe. Through a gap at the bottom I could see that the guard was seated to the left of the doorway. His chewing was the only sound from the hall. I paused, readying myself. I would get only one chance, and it had to be perfect.

With my left hand I swept back the curtain. With my right, I smashed the gourd down on the guard's temple. He turned as I swung, and I saw the look of surprise in his eyes just before they glazed over. He moaned and brought a weak hand to his head.

Wasting no time, I stumbled over him and sped along the hallway to the main door. I heard the guard call out "Stop!" weakly behind me, and I heard the clatter of his shield against the wall as he tried to follow.

At the entranceway I hesitated, but I had no time for rational decisions. I scurried down the steps and dashed across the courtyard to the only place that seemed to offer any protection: the construction in progress on the new palace.

I darted around one side, hoping that any observers would think I planned to continue down the street. Then I made my way among the piles of stone blocks and into the rubble-strewn foundations, searching for a hiding place. A series of waist-high retaining walls formed rectangles that would be filled with loose rocks to support the upper levels.

I heard shouts from the palace, but a glance back revealed no followers. Keeping low, I slithered over a retaining wall to the partially rubble-filled space beyond it. Crouched on rough stones, I pressed my back against the wall and gasped for breath. As my body cooled after my exertions, I began to shiver. I realized for the first time that I was naked.

I had run without thought of future action. Smoking Squirrel had once said that you have to act fast if taking the time to think would cause you to lose your chance. I had been thinking only about getting out of that terrible room, out of the palace Great Skull Zero had taken over. But now that I was free, a thousand difficulties assaulted me.

How would I get out of the city? Would Smoking Squirrel find out that I was free and take that message to my family? Did my parents still have their freedom, and could they leave without being stopped or followed? What about Feather Dawn? Where could I get some clothes?

This last, although seemingly the least important, was actually my most immediate problem. Even if I could skirt the guards, I could hardly wander through the streets of the city naked and not expect to attract attention. I would have liked a disguise, but at the very least I needed something to cover me, and I wasn't going to find it in an unfinished building.

I heard the echo of footsteps and curses from the courtyard. My curiosity overcame my fear for a moment and I peeked over the wall. Five or six guards had gathered and were gesturing frantically. They split up and began searching. One went back into the palace while others checked the kitchen building and dark corners. Two came toward me.

I ducked down and held my breath as I heard footsteps pass alongside the building and continue back to the gate. Anguished voices filtered through the air as the guards there denied having seen any runaway.

Before I could relax, I heard a curse nearby and a flaming torch bobbed above the outer wall of the new construction. One of the guards had broken off to search this area. The light dropped out of sight again and the guard swore furiously. I took advantage of his apparent stumble to slip over another retaining wall and put a few more feet between us.

I lay there in the dark, stretched along the wall and trying to make myself invisible. One small advantage was that my brown skin blended nicely with the shadows. Clouds generously covered Lady Moon, and I could barely see my own arms against the gray stone. If not for the torch, I would have been certain the guard couldn't find me unless he stepped on me.

Shadows flickered against the walls as the guard moved. Would he be careless and only glance in each compartment, or would he search thoroughly? Perhaps while he searched one section I could slip behind him to an area he'd already passed.

Then I noticed the courtyard wall, rising faintly in the darkness. It ran right alongside the construction on this side. Although the wall was much higher than my head, the retaining walls would give me a step up. If I could make it to the wall, I might be able to climb the rest of the way over. I wouldn't think about the drop down the other side, or what I might find in the street there.

I risked another peek over the wall. The guard's back was turned. I sensed more commotion in the courtyard but forced myself to ignore it. Take the chance when you have it, I thought, and crept on my hands and knees across the rubble toward the courtyard wall. The uncut stones gouged my bare skin, but I bit back the pain, kept one eye on the guard, and reached the next retaining wall.

After a swift glance around to check for observers, I swung my leg up, lay for a moment flat on my stomach on the wall, then put a hand and foot down on the other side and lowered myself once more into the safety of darkness. I listened to gauge the activity around me. The guard's torch flickered closer, grazing my shoulder with light.

The light dropped again, and I raised my head enough to see the guard bending to search a compartment nearby. He was so close I could see a bead of sweat running down the side of his face in the torch light.

I dropped down and squirmed across the rocks. Suddenly they shifted beneath me with a low groan. I lay frozen as the torch rose higher, the guard pausing silently. We waited patiently for each other, and finally he resumed his work.

The dozens of scratches along the front of my body were stinging from limestone dust, and my muscles ached with tension, but I had to continue. The facts were simple: move or die.

I reached the final retaining wall blocking my way and forced myself to wait calmly until the guard's back was turned before scrambling over the wall with less grace than I had used previously. The courtyard wall was little more than an arm's length away. I could have cried.

I took three slow, deep breaths before gently pushing myself up so I could see over the wall I had just crossed.

The guard was looking straight at me.

My arms went weak and I almost collapsed. Another warrior appeared at the far end of the construction and called out. The guard near me, holding the torch over his head, turned to answer. He had not seen me.

I couldn't hold back any longer. I rose to a crouch and took three waddling steps to the courtyard wall. One last look back. The guard had retreated to talk to his companion. The torch, held in front of him, silhouetted his broad back and flickered on the face of the other warrior.

I turned my attention to the wall. The limestone blocks had been cut smooth, fitted closely, and plastered over when the wall was built, but in the years since then the plaster had begun to peel, and the current construction had caused nicks.

When I stepped up on the retaining wall and stretched, I could just reach my fingers over the top of the courtyard wall. I searched for a foothold, spotted a crack near my right knee, and brushed loose pebbles out of it with my bare toes, then wedged those toes painfully into the tiny space.

I shifted my weight onto my right foot, clinging with my fingers for support. I started to lift my left leg, but my wedged toes slipped and a sharp pain shot through my left ankle as it landed hard on the retaining wall. I fell forward, slamming my face against the wall, and bit back a cry of pain.

I leaned against the wall, shaking, with warm blood oozing from my nose. I heard no shouts behind me, just the low murmuring voices of the guards in conversation.

Once more I crammed my toes into the crack. This time I did not stretch my fingers to the top of the wall. Instead I bent my left knee and lifted my arms over my head.

With a deep breath and every muscle straining, I pushed off with my left leg. I straightened my right leg, the precarious toehold supporting my weight for a moment. As I felt my foot slipping, I swung my arms over the top of the wall.

My arms and chin rested on the wall, supporting my dangling body. I struggled to pull myself up, thankful that I had not led a life of leisure and laziness. I wrested every drop of strength from my muscles, wriggling and straining until I could pull one and then both legs up onto the wall.

I lay on my stomach, panting, my arms folded close to my side, feeling the cool stone on my flushed skin. I must have made some sound during my struggles, because the two guards were approaching, looking alert and hopeful, aiming the light of their torches into the shadows between the retaining walls.

I didn't move and barely breathed. I pressed my lips tightly together and closed my eyes to slits so no glimmer of white would give me away.

I could have reached down and brushed my fingers against the hair of the guard who searched among the rubble beneath me, but he was looking around his feet and didn't raise his eyes.

I was afraid to move while they were so close, and anyway my body ached from scrapes, bruises, and the fall on my ankle. I dreaded even the thought of the long struggle of escape that still awaited. I would focus only on the next step.

Shouting from the courtyard attracted the guards' attention. I glanced up to see a tangle of people emerging from the temple. Great Skull Zero's head rose above them as they came down the steps.

The guards moved away from me, toward the edge of the construction. I slowly lifted my head and turned it so I could look down the other side of the wall, to freedom. The road was empty. The wall on that side was smooth; I would have to hang from my arms and then drop to the ground, hoping that my sore ankle would support me. I would have to move immediately, while the chance held.

"Eveningstar Macaw!"

Great Skull Zero's voice echoed through the quiet night. Sweat broke out on my forehead and I shuddered. He called my name again, and although I told myself to ignore him, I turned my head to look.

Great Skull Zero stood in the center of the courtyard, his brown skin shining in the torch light without its usual jeweled adornments. His black hair hung loose, spread out over his shoulders. His right hand held a long, black obsidian knife.

His left hand held Feather Dawn by the hair.

She knelt at his feet, her head forced back in his grip. Even at a distance I could see the whites of her eyes, huge with fear. Great Skull Zero pressed the blade against her slender throat.

"I will kill her right now if you do not come out."

The guards around the courtyard waited in silence. Great Skull Zero waited. Feather waited. I waited.

I would not give my life for hers. I owed her nothing. She was my sister, but she had ignored me, insulted me, betrayed me. She should welcome death if it meant an escape from her marriage to that demon. I would go on without her.

I was prevented from acting on my resolve by the trembling that seemed to have taken over my body and the tears that blurred my vision. I was amazed that the guards didn't somehow hear or feel me there. As the moments slipped away, I knew my opportunity was also slipping. The streets might already be filling with warriors called to join the search.

With a roar of anger, Great Skull Zero flung Feather from him. She sprawled on the pavement and scrambled to get away from him, but guards blocked her way.

"Go to her family's house," the high priest raged. "Bring her mother and father. Bring Double Bird. Bring the baby. I will kill them all."

"NO!"

The scream left my mouth before I could think. Great Skull Zero turned toward me, smiling. The two guards who had been searching the construction dragged me roughly off the wall. Carrying me clumsily between them, they stumbled over the rubble and across the courtyard, where they threw me at Great Skull Zero's feet.

I lay face down, sobbing, all hope gone out of me, my tears mixing with the blood and dirt on my face. A hand grabbed my hair and jerked me to my knees.

Great Skull Zero loomed over me with a malevolent smile.

"You will never win," he said softly. "I am the most powerful man in the city."

I stopped crying as I stared into his gleaming black eyes. My pain receded and a stillness settled over me.

"You may be the most powerful man," I said loudly, "but not the most powerful being. The gods will decide who wins. And who survives."

His eyes narrowed. "The gods," he hissed, then stopped, mouth open, as he saw the watching warriors around him. He calmed himself and spoke in a loud, steady voice, so all could hear.

"The gods will show whom they favor. Perhaps you will be the one to bring back the name of the new king."

He leaned down until his face was inches from mine, smiling viciously. "And when you do not survive," he whispered, "I shall send the rest of your family after you."

He released me with a shove that sent me sprawling and stormed off with a last command.

"Take her back to her room. And no more escapes!"

Two guards lifted me by my elbows. I saw Feather, still seated on the pavement, staring at me. Her wide, expressionless eyes met mine for a moment before I was dragged away.

 slept despite my fear and woke feeling that I'd just had strange and important dreams, but I was unable to remember what they were. My entire body ached and my nose was thick with clotted blood, forcing me to breathe through a dry, scratchy throat. As long as I could move, though, I would do so of my own power, so when the guards came for me well before daybreak, I climbed stiffly to my feet and met their gaze chin up and shoulders back, swaying only slightly.

They led me to the sweat baths, where silent young priestesses with frightened eyes washed me. They took pots of boiling water from the hearth and splashed them in hot stone troughs, sending a haze of white steam rising around us. The moisture cleared my nose and the intense heat soothed my sore muscles, but I also began to feel more awake and alert. I preferred the lethargy that had almost allowed me to ignore my fate.

In an outer chamber the priestesses dried me and painted my naked body blue, the color of sacrifice.

They combed my hair and twisted it around my head, holding it in place with slender bone pins. The older of the two brought out a long cloak of bright blue feathers and draped it gently over my shoulders, fastening it with a jade clasp above my right shoulder.

She picked up a bowl of dark liquid. "Drink this. It will ease your passage."

I knew the drink contained a drug that would put me into a trance, relaxing me so that I wouldn't scream or fight. Smoking Squirrel had used a large dose of it to knock out the guard when I tried to escape. I shook my head. I would accept my terror, if it gave me any small chance to fight for survival. The priestess was startled by my refusal, but she put the bowl aside.

She glanced at the doorway and the flickering shadows of torches as the bored guards mumbled to each other outside, then suddenly knelt before me and took my hand in her two soft ones.

"Please, when you get to the otherworld, beg the gods to help us," she whispered. "Tell them how frightened we are. The other sacrifices have done no good, but you are brave. Maybe they will listen to you."

I stared at her pleading eyes, then looked at the other priestess, who nodded to me anxiously. How could I explain that the gods had not seen fit to save me, so they would probably continue to ignore my

pleas? I hadn't gone through the proper period of fasting and ritual before sacrifice, so I didn't know which
part of the otherworld I would reach. I worried that I
would find myself in the terrible underworld, and not
the glorious upperworld at all.

"I will try," I said, and they gave me tiny smiles,
finding some small comfort.

The guards led me to the Temple of Itzamna,
where I spoke to Smoking Squirrel once more before
the ceremony. He gave me the final blessing, which
Great Skull Zero refused to do. The high priest
would, however, throw me into the well himself.

My gentle friend looked older than he had just the
day before, and his twisted back seemed to hurt him
more. Great Skull Zero had threatened him, but
Smoking Squirrel felt he was safe for a while longer.
He gave me the rites and then we stood together
looking out the doorway as the edges of the sky light-
ened. People were moving silently across the main
plaza, heading to the Well of Sacrifice.

I realized that I had not seen any stars overhead
and that the sky above was a dark slate gray. I thought
of Owl Scroll and her desperation to have the men
back before the first spring rain.

"Are you ready, my child?"

I looked at Smoking Squirrel and my eyes filled
with tears.

"I've tried so hard, and I haven't done any good. I

couldn't save Smoke Shell, or Feather, or even myself. Great Skull Zero will kill Double Bird's baby and probably my parents and you. I've ruined everything."

"No. Great Skull Zero has ruined everything."

"I should never have tried to fight at all," I insisted. "We are being punished by the gods, and you cannot fight that. What have we done to deserve such misery?"

Smoking Squirrel tapped his shoulder. "Did I do something to deserve this crooked back? I don't see how, as I was just a young child when I got sick. But perhaps the weakness in my body has made me stronger in spirit."

I stared at his lined face. "I'm not ready to die," I whispered. "I'm not that strong yet."

He put his arm gently around me. "Few people think themselves ready. But you are stronger than you know."

A procession entered the plaza below us. At that distance the marchers looked small as birds, and as brightly colored in their finery. I recognized Great Skull Zero by his size and by the green of jade and quetzal feathers that covered his body. He was being carried in a litter in the lead, and he was dressed like a king, missing only the jade headband and pendant that marked that highest office. The high priest was getting impatient.

With Smoking Squirrel at my side, I descended into the plaza to join the procession. When we reached them, my friend joined the priests trailing behind Great Skull Zero. The guards who had been watching me joined the warriors at the back of the party. I met the high priest's eyes for one moment of mutual hatred and then fell into step at his side and just behind him.

A special broad, white road led from the plaza to our destination. We walked through the city, joined by more people as they saw us pass, in the direction of the river. The Sacred Way led to a small stone temple.

A tributary to the river flowed underground at this point, and the limestone above it had collapsed to form a circular well as deep as four houses stacked on top of each other and as big across as a large court-yard. The rough, yellow limestone, streaked with black and dotted with clinging vines, went almost straight down to the dark green surface of the water. This was the Well of Sacrifice.

People lined the edge of the well when we arrived. My parents were as near to the temple as they could get, with four armed warriors nearby. My mother gave me a weak smile, then her lips continued to move in silent prayers. My father stood solemn beside her, and Small, tears staining his face, clutched a wooden statue almost as long as his arm. I was sure he had carved this piece to throw down as an offering with my sacrifice, and I was so touched I almost cried.

I would not give Great Skull Zero the satisfaction of my emotion, so I looked away from my family, studying the rest of the crowd. I saw Double Bird, her belly no longer swollen with pregnancy, standing with her family. I could not see the baby Smoke Shell. They were probably afraid that Great Skull Zero would make a last, quick addition to the sacrifice. I wanted to see my nephew just one time, but I hoped they had hidden the child safely.

At first I thought Feather Dawn had not come, but then she arrived, struggling against the guards who held her arms. She would witness her sister's death, a lesson to behave well for the man she would marry that very afternoon.

Great Skull Zero stepped up to the platform overlooking the well and raised his arms for silence. The somber crowd stilled completely, although they must have witnessed enough of these rituals to know every word.

"We come here today for a special purpose," the high priest began. "We are a city without a king. Our beloved King Flint Sky God, my dear friend, has left us without an heir. We ask the gods to give us the name of the man who is great enough, powerful enough, wise enough to be king. King Flint Sky God, who was like a brother to me, confided to me his concerns for his people. He asked me to watch over you through the troubled times ahead, and this I have done. But we need a proper king, and I pray that we will soon have one."

I seethed in anger as he droned on, beginning the long prayer that preceded the sacrifice. Surely no one was foolish enough to believe the high priest. I was becoming quite certain that the people saw Great Skull Zero's plot. Some were just too frightened to stop him, while others were receiving great rewards for siding with him.

I tried to maintain my anger, because it kept me from thinking about the next step in the ritual. I was reminded too soon, however, as Great Skull Zero called for me. Smoking Squirrel clasped my hand for a moment before the guards pushed me forward.

Two large young priests followed me. One removed the feather cloak from my shoulders and passed it back to the group behind us. I stood at the edge of the cliff, clean and naked except for the blue paint that covered my body, raging at my helplessness. One last time I looked around for my family. Mother. Father. Small. Double Bird. Feather Dawn. They stared back at me with large wet eyes. May the gods protect you, I thought.

Great Skull Zero gave a command. The young priests lifted me by my arms and legs. I struggled to keep calm, to hold back a scream, knowing that fighting would only dishonor me. The priests swung me back, then out over the edge of the Well of Sacrifice, releasing me in an arc over the cliff. I spun through the air, my limbs tangling. Instinctively, without knowing why, I drew my arms and legs in, curling into a tight ball. My dizzying fall seemed to take forever; with my eyes shut tight, I could only wait for the moment the water would hit me like a wall.

It came with a crash, and the breath I had been holding since the priests released me was forced out, paralyzing my ability to breathe and nearly knocking me unconscious.

I spun through the water, my limbs loose now, unable to think or act. Finally, as I slowed, I drew in a breath, and the water hit my lungs like searing flames. I began flailing then at the terror of surviving the impact of the water only to suffocate in the depths. I tried to control the demand to cough, as my legs propelled me upward, strengthened by a short life spent running through the jungle.

I broke the surface choking and crying, unable to see through the fog that filled my head. I was one of the few in our city who knew how to swim, from the trips to the coast with my father. I kicked my feet to keep my head afloat, snorting to clear my clogged nose and coughing through my burning throat.

Slowly my vision cleared and I got my bearings.

The cloudy water that had seemed hard as stone moments before now supported me gently. I had survived the fall! For a moment I felt pure joy.

The rough rock walls of the Well of Sacrifice rose almost straight up on all sides of the pool, broken only by clinging plants. A few feet away, a gold arm band began to sink below the surface of the water. I reached out to take this offering that some nobleman had thrown in after me. Everyone threw in some prize possession; most had already sunk.

I looked up, and as my eyes adjusted to the bright circle of light above me, I saw a ring of faces staring at me. Their excited murmurs filtered down but were soon cut off by the high priest's voice. His command echoed down to me.

"We must leave her to commune with the gods."

Reluctantly they moved off, and I thought I recognized the faces of my family among the last to disappear.

I had to survive until the priests returned at midday to see if I was still alive and to pull me out if I was. I didn't think I could last that long. My muscles, already sore from my nighttime escape, now burned from the exertion of keeping myself afloat. How long could I survive before I simply sank into the murky depths, choking against the water but unable to rise above it?

I saw something dark bobbing nearby and struggled to paddle my way over to it. The wooden statue Small had carved as an offering grinned at me. I drew it close in an embrace. The buoyant wood could not quite support my weight, but it allowed me to rest a little, keeping my head above water with just a few slow kicks. I wondered if Small had intentionally chosen a wood that floated and carved his statue so big. I thought that he probably had, giving me whatever small help he could, and I smiled for the first time that day.

The air above me was silent except for the calls of the birds. The people would be walking back to the city, to prepare for Feather's wedding to Great Skull Zero. I was alone. A lethargy began to overtake me. I knew I must do something, but I wanted only to sleep. I started to doze off but when I loosened my grip on Small's statue, it bobbed up to hit me in the chin.

I shook myself awake and looked around, hoping for some inspiration, and noticed the mist settling on my face. It was beginning to rain. Then I noticed two figures at the rim of the well. My hope soared for a moment, thinking my parents had come to rescue me. But they were too well guarded to sneak away unnoticed. These men wore the robes of priests.

They retreated, and I was surprisingly disappointed at the loss of the little company they provided. Then they appeared again, holding something between them. They tossed it out over the well, and as it unraveled against the gray sky, I saw that it was a rope. One end landed near me with a plop and began to sink.

I released the statue and swam to the rope, pulling myself forward with it until it settled straight down along the cliff.

"Tie it around yourself," one of the priests called.

I began to do as he said, then stopped as my joy at being rescued drained away. The priests were not supposed to return so early. And I recognized the voice as belonging to one of the young priests who had thrown me in the well. They did not mean to save me. They meant to kill me.

If they waited until the proper time to come for me, they might be joined by Smoking Squirrel and other honest priests who would insist that I be pulled up properly. So they came early, to ensure that my body would be settled in the bottom mud before anyone else could see that I had survived.

I let go of the rope. The priests waited above me. I had to get rid of them if I was to have any chance of escape.

"Are you ready?" one called.

"I can't," I said, making my voice weak and plaintive. "I've broken my arm, and I have no strength."

"You must."

"I feel so . . ." I let my voice trail off, then pushed out from the wall a little, floating on my side so they could see me. I took a slow, deep breath and let myself sink, releasing a few air bubbles. I fought to remain calm as the cold water closed around me. I peered through the foggy green and spotted a darker area that must be the wall.

I kicked slowly so as not to stir up the water and soon my outstretched arms touched the slimy moss of the cliff. Pressing close to it with a shiver, I raised my face just above the surface of the water. The clinging plants prevented a clear view of the top of the cliff. I gently propelled myself back a few feet to where a slight hollow in the rock surface and some thick hanging moss would further protect me from their sight.

"Hello?" one of the priests called.

We were all silent. I heard them mumbling to each other, then one came into view, circling along the edge of the well. I ducked my head and stayed down for as long as I could. When I finally had to come up, he was still there but looking across at his friend and calling to him.

"She's gone."

I took another breath, feeling dizzy, and sank again. When I rose, he was out of sight. A scraping noise startled me. The dangling rope jumped and danced nearby. The end flicked out of the water and began to rise. It had been too much to hope that they might leave it behind.

I watched the rope disappear, then waited to be sure they were gone. The rain came down harder, and I began to shiver. I could not stay here. Even if I could survive until the priests returned to officially check for me, I was sure they would find some way to kill me before I could speak out against Great Skull Zero. Surviving a sacrifice gave me great power, and he would not allow me to use it against him.

The cold kept me from feeling so tired, but I would have to act quickly or I would freeze. I stared up at the cliffs rising above me. The top seemed so far. I remembered how difficult it had been to climb just the short courtyard wall by the construction. The rock face here had not been cut by people, so it was uneven, but the surface had been worn smooth by the years, and now was slick with rain.

I had no choice. I would have to climb.

 paddled along the wall, looking for a place that offered some holds. I tried grabbing the clumps of moss, but they came off in my hands. The water seemed to pull me back whenever I tried to drag myself out, and my feet slipped off the small slime-covered ledges and bumps underwater.

I had circled most of the way around the well when I cracked my knee against a jutting piece of rock underwater. I folded forward at the pain and my gasp caught a mouthful of water, sending me into a fit of coughing.

When I could suck in clear air again, I felt for the rock. It slanted downward and didn't come out very far, but I scraped off the moss and managed to get my feet up on top of it and into fairly secure positions among the ridges. When I stood up, bracing myself against the wall, the water came only to my knees.

I blinked against the rain as I stared up the wall stretching away above me. I searched for holds with my eyes and my hands, pulling out plants to reveal the tiny cracks or ledges they sprouted from. Taking a deep breath, I lifted my right foot and wedged it sideways onto a bit of protruding stone. With my fingers clinging to an angled crack in the rock, I lifted my weight onto that foot, drawing myself completely out of the water.

I started to lean back to look above me, but the shift in weight was too much for my precarious foothold. I fell back into the water with a smack that left me stinging. I'll never make it, I thought, coughing against the water that filled my mouth. I felt more alone than I ever had. The well was as much of a prison as the king's tomb had been.

Through my tears I saw something small and pale bobbing in the water. I sniffled and wiped my eyes with a wet hand, then swam a few strokes to retrieve a small pouch made of deer gut. It was filled with air and tightly tied so that it floated. I swam back to the outcropping of rock and balanced myself on it while I opened my find.

A little water had seeped in, wetting the contents. I found a tortilla wrapped around some dried meat, and I tore into it hungrily, not caring that it was soggy in spots. Then I pulled out a small protective charm on a thin leather thong. Finally I dug out another smaller pouch of cloth. I recognized it as one of my mother's medicine bundles. It held a mix of seeds and herbs that would give the user energy and strength.

I began crying again, but this time out of gratefulness. I should have known that my mother would never give up on me. Well, I would repay her by not giving up on myself. I slipped the charm around my neck and spread the herbs in the remaining bit of tortilla, feeling better before they even had a chance to work.

I thought about waiting for the herbs to take full effect, but I was getting cold. Swimming had warmed me a little, but I would soon start to shiver if I stayed still. Shivering while climbing could mean shaking myself off the rock. If I kept swimming to warm myself, I might just get more tired. The rain seemed to have let up for the moment, but it might start again anytime, possibly much harder. I would begin immediately.

Once again I stood on the underwater outcropping of rock. Once again I found the small protruding rock, focusing on keeping my delicate balance. I sighed with relief as this step held. Now I only needed to do it again. And again. And again.

One step at a time. I found a bump for my other foot, then moved my hands higher. I crammed the toes of my right foot into a hole, then moved my left foot to the crack that had initially held my fingers. The smile left my face when I looked up and saw how much farther I must go.

Right hand. Left hand. Right foot. Left foot. Keep

the other three on the rock when moving one, for as much stability as possible. Just like climbing a tree. Search out every crevice, bump, indentation. Don't forget to breathe. Right hand. Left hand. Right foot. Left foot.

My arms ached so much they shook when I tried to lift them. My fingers cramped up so I could barely straighten them. I kept bumping my knees against the rock, until finally I learned to turn them outward when I lifted my legs. I was sure my toes were bleeding.

My hair had come loose and streamed out over my shoulders. Strands clung wetly to my face, but I forced myself to ignore them. Water dripped into my eyes and tickled the backs of my legs. The top was still so far away. I felt as if I hadn't moved at all.

I looked down over my shoulder to check my progress. Rain churned the surface of the water below. It seemed so far! With a gasp I turned back to the rock wall, clinging with every bit of strength left in my limbs as waves of dizziness and nausea swept over me.

I was shaking all over, and if I hadn't just found a particularly good hold for my right foot, I would have fallen for certain—fallen backward, spinning and flailing until I hit the hard surface of the water, never to rise again.

I pushed such thoughts out of my mind. If the water was so far below me, then the top must not be so far above. I took a few deep breaths, then found another foothold, creeping up the side of the lime-stone well one step or grasp at a time.

Right hand. Left hand. Right foot. Left foot. My mind began to wander, flickering over events of the past months. Great Skull Zero seemed to laugh at me, saying, "You'll never make it! I will be king." Then my mother's face intruded, and she held out her hands to me, beckoning me higher. A wooden statue with Small's face smiled and said, "For luck!"

My hand slipped off a mossy ledge and I wobbled, feeling my stomach drop away from me. I scrabbled for the hold and regained my balance, panting heavi-ly. I had been careless and had not cleared off the ledge before trusting my fingers to it. I must not let my mind wander.

The rim of the well was tantalizingly close. I did not look back to see how far I had come. Only a few more steps and I would be out, but the rock was smoother here, worn down by wind as well as rain, and the few bumps and ridges seemed far too small to hold me, especially as they were slick with moisture.

The thought of falling back into the well reared up in my mind, filling me with terror. I clung to the rock, afraid to move, certain that if I let go for even an instant I would slip and plummet to my death. My breath came short and fast, and I leaned my forehead against the rock, closing my eyes and trying to let the terror slide away.

I allowed myself to picture my mother again, without letting the daydream distract me too much. Her lips were moving, and I knew she was praying for me. Prayer was useless, I thought. The gods had forsaken me.

When I tried to save my brother, I was trapped in a tomb. I was captured by Great Skull Zero the day after I returned home. When I escaped from the temple, I went in the wrong direction and ran straight into the high priest. When I escaped again, I was captured again. Nothing had gone right. I had failed every time.

But I was alive.

Despite everything, I was alive. I remembered what Smoking Squirrel had said about his twisted back making his spirit stronger. Either the gods were testing me, in which case killing me now would be a pointless kind of joke, or else they didn't care what happened to me. Either way, I had nothing to gain by hanging on to a rock cliff like a clinging plant. Sooner or later my fingers would give out and I would fall to my death for sure. I expected it would be sooner.

I would trust in the gods, and in myself, and know soon enough if I was right. I ran my right hand over the slick stone, searching for anything to grip. A little blue flower sprouted from the rock just within my reach, and I ruthlessly dug it out and let it fall to the water below. I explored with my fingers and found that I could jam two of them in past the first knuckle.

I searched with my left foot for another hold. I was afraid to use my eyes, because a glance down would show me the surface of the water and I wasn't sure I could fight back that panic again. I found a slight ridge. Would it hold?

I needed to find a hold for my other foot before I trusted my weight on what I had now. I risked looking down, locking my eyes on the wall in front of me, and saw just to the right a ledge I had used shortly before for my hand. I remembered that it was fairly deep.

Keeping my eyes on that spot, I forced my fingers even farther into their hole, took a breath, tensed my muscles, and in one smooth step brought my right foot up to the ledge and shifted my weight to it even as my left foot slipped.

I could find no solid hold for my left hand and had to be satisfied with bracing it against the rock while I brought my left foot up to where my left hand had just been. I then brought my right foot up to join it.

I reached up with my left hand to the rim of the well and wrapped my fingers around some stone. My heart was pounding, but I forced myself not to rush. I had come too far to make a mistake now.

I pulled on the rock, testing its solidity. Suddenly it

came away in my hand. My balance shifted backward as bits of rock and dirt rained down in my face. I grabbed for another hold, dropping the rock. It bounced painfully against my shoulder before clattering against the limestone wall on its way down.

I blinked my eyes to clear the stinging grit, and I felt flooded with relief that I was still there to do so. My left hand clung to the hole where that rock had been, and this hold seemed solid enough. I needed one more step on my way up, then I was able to put my right forearm over the rim of the well. I dragged myself up, straining my exhausted arms, until I lay with my upper body on stable ground and my legs dangling over the edge.

Not a single part of my body was free of pain, but I lay face down on the hard rock in the rain with my arms stretched out as if embracing the whole solid, flat world.

Sometime later I was able to roll over and pull my legs up with the rest of me. I stared up at the dark gray sky and let the rain wash over me, cleaning away the dirt and blood and remains of blue paint.

Finally I sighed and sat up weakly. I would have liked to stay right there and sleep through the rainy season. But the priests would return for their official check anytime, and I didn't want them to find me there. I needed some time to think and plan.

I shifted onto my hands and knees and peered out over the cliff at the long wall I had just climbed and the dark surface of the water below. Shuddering, I drew back, but I was pleased. I had survived the Well of Sacrifice.

Painfully I struggled to my feet and took a few shaky steps. I realized I was ravenously hungry. The little stone temple at the edge of the well was nearby, and I wobbled toward it. Then I heard laughter.

I froze, trying to identify the direction of the sound. I could see no one, but I realized someone must be in the temple. Crouching down, I went the rest of the way on hands and knees. Steps led up alongside the temple to the platform in front, where the priests had thrown me into the water. The doorway of the temple was there, facing the Well of Sacrifice. I noticed a couple of spears leaning alongside the doorway. Great Skull Zero must have left guards behind, and they had taken shelter from the rain.

Crawling around the temple, I reached the white ceremonial road. The temple had no windows at the back, so I would be out of sight of the guards so long as they stayed inside. I stood and began walking back to the city.

I needed food, clothing, and someplace to dry off.

I could not go home, in case guards were still there. The Temple of Ix Chel was near. I would go there.

I passed by quiet houses and other small temples without thinking about much of anything but putting one leg in front of the other. If I had been confronted, I wouldn't have had any fight left in me. I was also naked and dripping wet, which would have made it hard to pass anyone unnoticed, but the streets in the area seemed deserted. Everyone must have gone to the plaza for the wedding ceremony.

I reached the temple and paused outside. The flight of stairs was only about as tall as me, but to my weary legs it seemed endless. I remembered another time I had come here in trouble, the day before Smoke Shell died. It seemed so long ago that I could hardly believe I was living the same life.

When I thought of Smoke Shell, I found it hard to remember him as my brother, the man who had swung me around in his arms and taught me to read and count and watched with pride while I let blood with his obsidian knife. He had become both more and less than that, a legend, a hero, not a thing of comfort, but a thing of awe.

I wished Small were there with me. The urge came on suddenly, painfully, perhaps brought on by the memory of how he had waited for me, huddling cloakless in the cool rain, while I went to pray over Smoke Shell's coming death. He had done so much for me, unasked and unrewarded, and if he had been there, I would have thrown myself in his arms and cried.

Instead I held back the tears and mounted the temple steps. I realized that Mother and Small could not have even tried to rescue me, because of the guards—those waiting at the Well of Sacrifice and those that must surround them at that moment. Although it seemed obvious that no one could have rescued me, in the back of my mind I had been hurt and angry that they had not come to help. But they didn't even know I was still alive.

I stood blinking in the dim temple. I wanted only to curl up someplace warm and sleep, but I was beginning to realize, horribly, that my work had just begun. Feather Dawn would soon be married to Great Skull Zero if I didn't stop them. I was tempted to let her suffer a little more first, but other people would be suffering, too.

What's more, I knew that this was my best opportunity to stop Great Skull Zero once and for all.

A girl stood at the entrance to a poorly lighted passageway, staring at me with huge dark eyes. "It's you," she whispered, her voice trembling.

She was nine or ten, an ordinary girl, apparently a temple priestess. I didn't recognize her, and I wondered how she knew me and why she was scared. Then I started to smile, but quickly hid it, stretching proudly to my full height, which was at least a hand or so taller than hers, and frowning.

"Yes, it is I, Eveningstar Macaw. I have come back from the Well of Sacrifice with a message from the gods."

She gave a little shriek, her hands fluttering. "But why are you here? Why aren't you with the priests who pulled you out?"

I considered and decided I had no reason not to tell the truth. "The priests are not all honest. I did not wait for them. I came up alone."

"But how? It's not possible!"

"Anything is possible when you have the favor of the gods."

Well, it wouldn't hurt to be a little vague. Let her think Itzamna himself had lifted me gently in his hands. I took charge with all the imperiousness appropriate to someone who had survived the Well of Sacrifice. I was beginning to form a plan.

"I need some clothes. The best you can find. And bring me some mica powder and yellow ocher."

"I don't think we have any here."

"Then find some," I snapped. "Hurry, and don't tell anyone that I'm here. Go on. I'll make sure the fire doesn't go out while you're gone. And bring me some food, too!"

She scuttled out on her errand, and I sank onto my knees in front of the altar. Fighting back exhaustion, I raised my eyes to the image of Ix Chel, moon goddess, Lady Rainbow, Mother of All. Goddess of my mother and my grandmother, my sister and myself.

"Please," I prayed, "Great Skull Zero must be punished for all his crimes. He is no longer a man of the gods, he is corrupt and cruel, and our city suffers much because of him. Help me, please, to know what is right and to do what is right."

I sat for some time in the darkness, waiting for a sign.

By the time the girl came back, I knew exactly what I must do.

he plaza was crowded with people. I paused at the corner of a building, nervously adjusting my shawl and smoothing my hair. I would have liked a nice long sweat bath, but this was not a day for indulgences. The rain had left me reasonably clean, and the skirt and shawl covered most of my scrapes and bruises. In fact, I thought wryly, people would be unlikely to recognize me at a glance, because I was dressed so much more nicely than I usually was.

The girl, Red Sea Turtle, had known all about the wedding plans. Once I got her to relax enough to talk to me, she related them with self-pitying sighs because she could not attend. My sudden appearance had added a definite dose of excitement to her day, but in her young mind nothing beat the enchantment of a royal wedding.

Despite all that I had been through, it was just midday, and the ceremony was about to begin. Usually widowed or divorced people, like Great Skull Zero, wouldn't have a ceremony for a new wedding. They would just begin to live with their new spouse and invite all their friends to a banquet in celebration.

But Feather had never been married before, and more importantly, Great Skull Zero wanted everyone to see and recognize this marriage. He wanted everyone to know that he had married the sister of a hero, because he thought it would help his bid for the kingship. The entire city had been invited to witness the ceremony.

I slipped around the edges of the crowd until I came to the plaza entrance where the wedding party would pass. Already I could hear the musicians coming up the street, as I wedged myself against a wall, just behind the front row of viewers.

I had a moment to study the people around me. I saw farmers from the villages, given a break from their labors on Great Skull Zero's new temples and palace, along with artisans, minor officials, and local laborers. Everyone should have been excited about participating in a royal ceremony, but I saw concern and even fear in the strained faces that glistened with moisture from the rain. The children seemed to sense their elders' silent thoughts; they stood solemn and quiet or clung to their mothers, crying.

I smiled. The people were ready for me.

The musicians arrived in a clamor, playing drums, blowing whistles, or shaking shell rattles. The noise seemed jarring and random, as if the players' hearts weren't in their music.

Long rows of warriors, four abreast, came next. I studied the immobile faces, which didn't flinch even when raindrops trickled down their noses, and wondered if these people were loyal to the high priest. I guessed that Great Skull Zero would have posted the most loyal guards around the plaza and at his destination, the Temple of Itzamna, with a few accompanying him along the way. The rest of the guards were probably just following orders from the one person powerful enough to give them.

The priests followed, in a more ragged bunch than the warriors. Smoking Squirrel was among them, his lips moving in a prayer, not, I thought, for the happiness of this marriage, but for the safety of Feather's soul. He looked up at me as if he felt my gaze on him, and our eyes met. I held my breath, but he kept walking, without missing a step, his expression giving no indication of what he had seen.

I would have to be more careful, I realized, and when the engaged couple finally came into view, I ducked back so that my sister and the high priest would not see me. Great Skull Zero was dressed in all the glory of a king, and I fumed when I saw the royal jade breastplate hanging across his chest, prominent even among the gold and quetzal feathers that dripped from his body and shone despite the rain.

Feather Dawn walked a few paces behind. She stood tall, her gaze up, her damp face expressionless, her eyes clear and dry. She did not look like a happy bride on her wedding day, but she did look as if she could be queen, and I was suddenly proud. She was, after all, the daughter of my mother and father, the sister of my brother and me. She was showing a strength and pride I hadn't known she possessed.

At the end of the procession was a row of about twenty maidens, beautiful noble priestesses chanting softly. As they passed, the crowd around me turned to watch the group proceed through the courtyard, and with a pounding heart I slipped from my place and joined the row of young women.

The clattering musicians had already crossed the plaza and were about to ascend the temple stairs, their awkward music carrying easily even in the moist air. I dared not look around for fear of catching someone's eye and being recognized, but I sensed something strange about the crowd. I was halfway across the plaza before I realized what it was, or rather, what it wasn't. No one was talking, or cheering, or throwing out praises to the high priest. The only noises were the musicians and the faint wails of crying children.

The soldiers broke off as they climbed the steps, forming double rows along each side. They faced the crowd, weight evenly centered over slightly spread legs, both hands clasping their spears in front of them, faces blank. Following the priests, Great Skull Zero and Feather continued their stately walk between the rows of warriors, and I prayed that the maidens would follow them. My plan depended on getting to the top unnoticed.

By the time the priests had spread out across the top platform, I was stepping onto the stairs, my heart thumping loud enough to drown out the musicians. When the maidens began reaching the top, they split off, one to the right, the next to the left, forming a pretty row across the platform, just in front of the temple façade. I passed within two arms' lengths of the wedding couple, but caught in their own thoughts, they did not notice me. As I was at the end of the line, I wound up right in the middle of the façade, in front of the temple doorway. The girl just in front of me glanced at me in puzzlement, but we had never met, and she said nothing.

I was just about to sneak into the temple when I heard movement coming from there. I ducked my head away as a group came out, brushing by my shoulder. As I peeked out from under lowered eyelids, a jolt ran through my body. My parents were being pushed forward by four guards with drawn knives. I almost cried out, but remembered my mission in time. They stood, angry and helpless, just behind Feather. They would show their support of this marriage whether they liked it or not.

All eyes turned forward as Great Skull Zero stepped to the top of the stairs and addressed the crowd in his booming voice, beginning a long speech praising the gods and himself. I didn't wait to hear it. Instead I edged backward, into the temple.

A man waited there in the gloom. I froze, my stomach twisting, but I couldn't stop there. He had not yet seen me, as he was facing the wall and leaning against it, resting his face on folded arms. I drew my obsidian knife and crept forward, telling myself that I must do this thing, even if it meant killing somebody.

When I was close enough to touch him, I paused. I lifted my knife but my hand was shaking and I let it drop. Maybe I could just hit him with the flat of the knife and knock him unconscious. But if I didn't hit hard enough, he could give me away.

As I hesitated, struggling over what I must do and could not do, I noticed something. This man was not a warrior, but wore a simple tan cloak. Even in the darkness, his anguish was visible in every line of his body, and I sensed something familiar about him. Before I knew it, I had spoken, in a low whisper.

"Small?"

He spun around, his mouth open, and I barely had time to clasp my hand over it before he could speak. He pulled me to him, wrapping his arms around me tightly and burying his face against my hair. My knife fell to the floor with a thud, but I could not even turn to see if anyone had heard. I returned Small's embrace, trying not to laugh or cry out loud.

Finally he loosened his grip a little, raising one hand to stroke my cheek with his thumb and staring at me with a dazzling smile. Then he leaned forward and kissed me.

A shock like lightning shot through my body as his lips touched mine. When he pulled away, we stared at each other in confusion. He released me suddenly and stumbled over the words of an apology. I didn't have time to think about what this meant, and as he spoke I remembered our need for silence. I lay my fingers gently over his mouth and gestured to the doorway. He nodded, and I covered our embarrassment by getting to work.

With only the murals of Itzamna to see us, I pulled containers from my waistband and Small helped me paint my face in yellow ocher and sparkling mica powder like that worn in ceremonies by royalty, the chosen ones of the gods. I exchanged the decorative headband I wore for the one I had borrowed from the priestess of Ix Chel, which bore the moon goddess's distinctive pattern.

With a last nervous press of Small's hand, I warned him to wait there. Then I adjusted my skirt and shawl, took a deep breath, and prepared to confront the most powerful and dangerous man in the city.

reat Skull Zero was directly in front of me as I stepped from the temple, but he was looking out over the plaza. Feather Dawn knelt to his left, facing him, head bowed, and my parents stood next to her, clutching each other's arms, looking strained. The drizzle had stopped, and the gray skies were painfully bright after the gloom of the temple interior.

A voice in my head said, "It is fated," and I was unafraid.

The maidens along the wall were the first to see me as I passed them. They stirred, and a few gasped, attracting the attention of the priests and musicians who mingled just in front of them. From the corner of my eye I saw Smoking Squirrel smile, a great, beautiful smile that erased the crookedness from his features. I kept my own face calm as I stepped forward.

A gasp from my mother told me that she had seen. She swayed and leaned on my father. Feather lifted her eyes and stared at me, uncomprehending, as I stepped between her and the high priest, who was still rambling along in his booming monologue. Murmurs rose from the crowd below, and behind me, girls gasped. Great Skull Zero hesitated as he finally sensed something happening. I took that moment to speak, projecting my voice as a drum throws its music through the air.

"Stop," I shouted, so all in the plaza could hear.

Great Skull Zero gave a high-pitched squeal and stumbled away from me, the blood draining from under his dark skin and leaving him strangely pale.

"This dawn, I, Eveningstar Macaw, was cast into the Well of Sacrifice. I have returned with a message from the gods."

The crowd was immediately silent, and an energy stronger than the sun seemed to connect me with every one of them. Around me, priests fell to their knees in prayer. Great Skull Zero screamed, "Kill her! Kill her!" but the guards waited, motionless, looking back and forth between us. My voice was clear and calm as I spoke.

"The gods are angry."

Moaning wails. This they could easily believe.

"We are a city without a king. Without a leader. One man plans to be our king."

I turned to Great Skull Zero. His shock was fading, his features settling into the hardness of hatred. For a moment I felt a tremor of fear, and I remembered all the times I had challenged him—and failed.

"Great Skull Zero is not our rightful king." I shouted even louder, to drown my fear.

He stepped toward me with a snarl. "There is no other," he yelled. "Let one man come forward who would be king."

Silence settled over the crowd. No one had the courage to confront the high priest yet. And no one had the knowledge or power to be king. Great Skull Zero began to regain his confidence, straightening to his full height two heads above me with a smug smile. He opened his mouth, and I cut him off.

"The high priest is right. He has made certain that no one else lives to challenge him. And we have let him commit his evil deeds, so we are at fault, too."

You let him, I wanted to say. *I* have been doing my best to stop him. But this was no time for bragging or scolding.

"The gods have commanded us. Itzamna, Ix Chel, Chac, Yam Kax, Ah Puch, Ah Kinchil, Hunab Ku." I recited the litany of holy names to impress them with the divinity of my message. My next instructions would not be easy.

"We have let the high priest destroy our city. So we are a city no more." I paused. "We must leave the city. The gods have told me. We must walk away from this place of evil. We have forgotten the Mayan way. We must learn again, starting with nothing. Farmers! Return to your villages while there is still time to save the crops. You are needed there. The rest of you must find other cities—"

The intent silence around me was broken by an animal howl. I turned to see Great Skull Zero bearing down on me with knife drawn.

I tried to run but could not turn fast enough. I stumbled and fell, the blade slicing the air in a line directly to my heart. I closed my eyes.

But instead of a cold stone blade hitting my chest, a warm, hard body slammed against me. I gasped as the air was knocked out of me, then opened my eyes to see Small sprawled against my chest, a black knife protruding from his shoulder.

Great Skull Zero grabbed the knife again and pulled it out with a grunt, releasing a gush of blood. Small gasped and a spasm shot through his body. I clung to him, trying to drag us both out of the way as the knife rose again. I tried to scream but choked on the sound.

I felt hands reaching for me, pulling me, and then a figure broke off from the group of priests in a blur, holding his own black dagger. As Great Skull Zero lunged forward, Smoking Squirrel brought his knife down in a wild slash, catching the high priest across the face and neck.

My parents and sister pulled me out of the way as Great Skull Zero fell, and his weapon clattered harmlessly by my feet. He sprawled on the stone steps with a horrible rasping gasp, flailing wildly. Smoking Squirrel stood above us, half his face looking shocked and the other half looking proud of what he had done. The rest of us clung to each other in a jumbled heap, neither moving nor speaking. The air around us was silent.

A warrior stepped toward the high priest and looked down on him for a moment. Then he shoved his foot into Great Skull Zero's fleshy side. The body began to tumble down the steps, and other cheering warriors moved forward to help it on its way.

Small groaned. Mother sprang into action, instructing my father to help her as they lifted him off of me and tried to stop the bleeding. Feather Dawn smiled shyly at me and went to help them, offering her beautiful woven belt as a bandage. Smoking Squirrel dropped his knife and held out a hand to help me to my feet.

I stood just as the high priest's body reached the base of the temple steps. The crowd exploded with noise and activity. The soldiers on the steps began dropping to their knees and bowing their foreheads to the ground in my direction. No doubt some who had been loyal to Great Skull Zero were now concerned about their own fate, but I like to think that some were also bowing in honest gestures of respect and admiration.

The maidens began kneeling, too, confused and breathless, and the musicians joined them. Smoking Squirrel, still holding my hand, bowed low before me. Then each of the other priests came forward and bowed in turn, as the crowd below roared its praise. They were already beginning to deface the huge tree-stone that Great Skull Zero had been building for himself, breaking off the high priest's image in chunks with whatever tools they could find.

In my heart I knew that soon my earlier words would

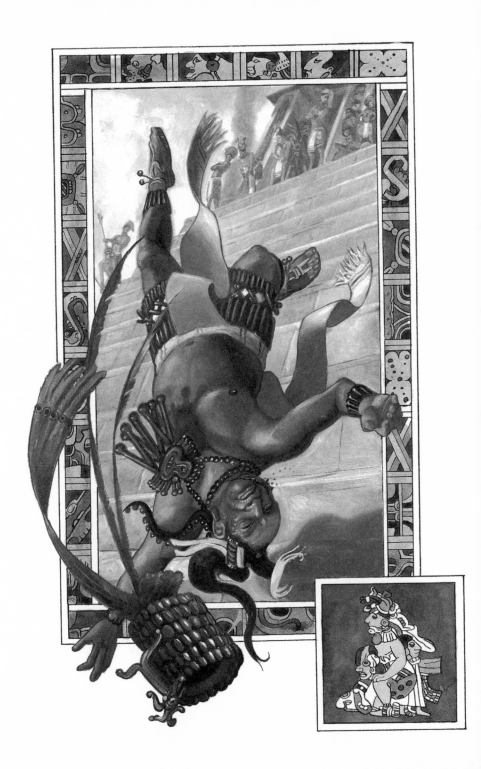

sink in and the joy of many would be replaced by confusion and desperation. The farmers would suffer the least, although the villages would have to quickly align themselves with some other kingdom for protection. The artisans, merchants, and other professionals could find work in other cities, and laborers were always needed. The priests would be taken in by their counterparts in other kingdoms.

The nobles . . . I did not know what the nobles would do. Other cities would have nobles of their own and would be unlikely to welcome ours with gifts of land and goods in exchange for little real work. But the nobles had helped bring this fate on themselves with their greed and indifference. They would find some way to survive, or else they would die.

For now, though, the people were caught up in the excitement of freedom. A great spontaneous celebration was already beginning. The musicians began to play as they marched down the temple steps, and this time their music was rich and enthusiastic. The group snaked through the plaza and the crowd began dancing. The storehouse doors were broken open and the ingredients of a feast dragged from them.

I let them go about their business. I had done my duty to the gods and my city, and at that moment I cared about only one thing, my dear wounded friend. I joined the group gathered around him. Small was sitting up, pale but breathing. Mother was binding his shoulder with strips of cloth while Feather held the bandage in place. I knelt beside him and took his hands in mine.

When Mother was finished, she reached across to stroke my hair. We had so many things to say, so many explanations, so many stories, but they could all wait. For that moment the joy of being a family again was all we needed.

Smoking Squirrel joined us, and Mother held out her hand to him, saying simply, "My friend."

She turned to Small. "You have the courage of ten warriors. I give you your freedom, something you deserved long ago. You are no longer a servant, but a member of this family, welcome to stay with us for as long as you choose. I would also like to give you a new name. You have protected my daughter from so many dangers. I give you the name Shield."

one of us felt like joining the crowds—not even Feather Dawn. We slipped out of the plaza as quietly as possible and returned to the home I had seen so seldom in recent months. As we walked through empty streets, the euphoria of success began to drain away, and I wanted nothing more than to go to bed.

Instead, we talked late into the night, revived by soothing hot atole, whatever food Mother and Feather Dawn could throw together, and, for me, some herbs from Mother's medicine basket to relax my aching muscles.

Double Bird joined us, carrying the baby Smoke Shell, and I got to hold my squirming, gurgling nephew for the first time. Double Bird's face filled with joy when she looked at her child, and although she spoke of my brother with sadness, she had gotten over the worst of the pain.

Finally, reluctantly, we turned the talk from stories of the recent past to plans for the future. We debated every option, discussing the merits of each city where we might be welcomed.

"Must we leave, really?" Feather Dawn asked. "Can't the city be saved somehow?"

They all looked at me. I shook my head slowly. "King Flint Sky God was a good man, but not as strong a ruler as he should have been. Now Great Skull Zero has destroyed whatever chance the city might have had under a new king."

I looked at the dwindling stack of tortillas between us and thought of Owl Scroll in her farm hut. "We have no food. Without food, nothing else matters. We can't even defend ourselves from the attacks of other cities."

"It would take years to fill the storehouses again," Smoking Squirrel said. "Even if nobody took food out."

I nodded. "Maybe in a few years we could build back up, if we had a good leader. A weak king, or one who didn't know what he was doing, would just make things worse."

"*You* could lead," Feather said.

I stared at her with my mouth open, then grinned. She smiled back, blushing. "No, thanks," I said. "I've had enough for a while. I just want to go back to leading a normal life."

Mother smiled mischievously. "You won't like it," she said. "You'll be getting into trouble again before your fifteenth birthday. I don't need to be an interpreter to see that."

I grudgingly laughed along with the others. "I don't see how I could top this," I said. "I suppose I could go around to other cities, preaching rebellion wherever I saw people mistreated. . . ." My voice trailed off as I imagined helping the farmers and other poor throughout the region. Surely other cities suffered under cruel leaders. I quickly shook off my reverie and joined back in the laughter.

In the end, we decided to head for Saymal, a coastal city to the northeast. My father had business contacts there and would be able to renew his trade. Feather Dawn would find the civilization she craved, a market for her textiles, and in time, no doubt, a good husband. Double Bird thought it likely her family would agree to settle there, as she had some cousins in the city. Smoking Squirrel would join us, too; he had no close family to follow.

Mother would find many uses for her talents in the city and the poorer villages nearby. I could join her on her medicinal rounds, perfecting my own skills, and I loved the thought of being near the ocean.

We ran out of words at last and tumbled into our beds. Strangely, I could not sleep. I stared into the darkness as the sounds of breathing slowed around me, then slid out of bed, pulled a blanket around my shoulders, and stole into the courtyard.

I knelt before our shrine, studying every detail of the symbols of Ix Chel. I knew that we would continue to need her in the days ahead, but I couldn't find the words for prayers. Finally, I simply whispered, "Thank you."

When I turned to go in, I saw that Small had followed me and was leaning against the wall, watching.

He came across the courtyard to meet me. We stood facing each other, the dawn just beginning to light our features, and it was some time before he spoke.

"I've been wanting to talk to you all night. I am free, now . . ."

Small—Shield, now—had sat silent throughout the earlier discussion, offering no suggestions or complaints. I had not thought to wonder if he would choose to go with us, but he was free and could do whatever he pleased.

"You will stay with us, won't you?" I asked, my heart aching at the thought of losing him. "Please, won't you come—not as a servant or a helper, but as . . . as a friend."

"I will go where you are," he said, taking my hands. "For as long as you will have me."

"Always," I answered. I leaned into his chest and we held each other, forgetting for a moment the trouble and work that still lay ahead.

AUTHOR'S NOTE

In the ninth century A.D. Europe was in the Dark Ages, with small feudal states where poor peasants worked for independent lords. Christianity was spreading across Europe while Islam extended throughout the Middle East and Spain. Maps showed only Europe, northern Africa, the Middle East, and parts of Asia. Most Europeans thought the earth was flat, and that the Atlantic and Pacific oceans were the borders of the world. They had no idea that North and South American even existed. Christopher Columbus's voyage was six hundred years in the future.

In the ninth century A.D. the Mayan civilization was at its height. The empire that began to flourish around A.D. 300 had grown to include over one hundred city-states, some with fifty thousand people. The Mayan world covered what is today southern Mexico and the Yucatán peninsula, Guatemala, Belize, and parts of Honduras and El Salvador. According to Mayan mythology, the gods made the first people from corn. However, like other Native Americans, the ancestors of the Maya probably migrated from Asia over a land bridge thousands of years ago. By 2000 B.C. they had reached Central America.

They had no metal tools or draft animals, and they used wheels only on toys. Yet they built hundred-foot-high temples from stone that was brought miles through the jungle. Cities hundreds of miles away from one another traded goods such as salt, honey, obsidian, and cotton. The Maya cut down dense forests and made rocky ground fertile with advanced farming techniques such as terraces and irrigation canals. They charted the paths of the stars and developed a calendar more complex than ours today. Their number system used zero centuries before Europeans learned the concept.

Priests ruled the Mayan cities and built great temples to show off their power. They claimed the ability to communicate with the gods, through bloodletting ceremonies and sacrifices such as the ones Eveningstar witnessed. The people believed that human blood fed the gods and earned their goodwill. They gods were complex and sometimes dangerous—Chac brought life-giving rain, but other gods were associated with drought, starvation, and war. The priests were also the nobility and the government, and were led by the Halach Uinic, the "true man" or king. This position was inherited by his eldest son.

Most Mayan girls lived quiet, simple lives. Growing up, they learned weaving and housekeeping from their mothers. When they were old enough to marry, they started families of their own. Many died young, during childbirth or from disease. Eveningstar would have been unusual in any time and place. Yet every culture produces a few rare people like Eveningstar, whose courage and determination change society.

Around A.D. 900, Mayan civilization collapsed. Many great cities were abandoned, seemingly overnight. Nobody really knows why. Some theories suggest earthquakes, disease, foreign invasion, or civil war. Most likely, the cities simply got too big and could no longer support themselves when overfarming depleted the soil. Perhaps a combination of events was to blame.

The Maya continued to build new cities, mostly in Mexico's Yucatán peninsula, where they mixed with the Toltec people from central Mexico. But their golden age had ended. By the time Europeans explored the Americas in the sixteenth century, most Mayan cities were deserted and covered by jungle, and the Mayan people were scattered throughout independent provinces. Though they resisted Spanish invaders, they were slowly conquered, except for a few who retreated to hidden settlements deep in the jungle. Millions died from diseases brought by the Europeans, while Spanish missionaries destroyed many clues to Mayan culture, including all the books they could find.

Some cities were completely destroyed and rebuilt by the Spanish. Other Mayan cities were abandoned and forgotten. The jungle took over, covering the great temples and palaces with earth and plants. In the early nineteenth century the word *Maya* did not appear in the dictionary. Then in 1839, an American, John Lloyd Stephens, and an English artist, Frederick Catherwood, explored Mayan ruins throughout Mexico and Central America. The illustrated books they wrote about their travels were bestsellers and inspired other explorers. Eventually archeologists and anthropologists began to probe the secrets of the ancient Maya, clearing away the jungle and rebuilding the great temples. They are still at work.

Today several million Maya, speaking at least thirty different Mayan dialects, live throughout Latin America. They live mostly in small farming villages, growing cotton, corn, beans, and squash as their ancestors did. Many other Mexicans and Central Americans have a mix of Mayan and Spanish blood.

The fictional city where Eveningstar lived is located approximately where Mexico, Guatemala, and Belize meet. The characters' names are translations of hieroglyphic names found on monuments and murals, while the gods' names are given in Mayan. Although scholars have learned a great deal about ancient Maya culture and history, we know very little about specific Mayan individuals of the past. The characters and events in *The Well of Sacrifice* are all fictional, but I have tried to make the setting and customs as accurate as possible. This story is one way of imagining how a great Mayan city may have been abandoned.